A King Production presents…

Baller Bitches
THE REUNION
VOLUME 4

A NOVEL

JOY DEJA KING

ISBN 13: 978-1942217329
ISBN 10: 1-942217-32-3
Cover concept by Joy Deja King.

Library of Congress Cataloging-in-Publication Data;
King, Deja Joy
Editor: Jacqueline Ruiz: tinx518@aol.com
Baller Bitches The Reunion: a series/by Joy Deja King
For complete Library of Congress Copyright info visit;
www.joydejaking.com Twitter: @joydejaking

A King Production
P.O. Box 912, Collierville, TN 38027

A King Production and the above portrayal logo are trademarks of A King Production LLC

"Friendship Is Like Money, Easier Made Than Kept."

~Samuel Butler~

This Book is Dedicated To My:

Family, Readers, and Supporters.
I LOVE you guys so much. Please believe that!!

A KING PRODUCTION

Baller
Bitches
THE REUNION
VOLUME 4

HOLLYWOOD

JOY DEJA KING

Chapter One

Nothing Seems To Be The Same

The gray skies filled with heavy clouds on the cold winter day satirized the grief looming in the air. The low rumble of distant thunder could be heard as guests arrived for the outdoor graveside funeral service.

"Do you think Blair and Kennedy are coming?" Diamond asked Cameron as they took their seats.

"Honestly..."

"Look," Diamond cut her husband off as she nodded her head towards the arriving cars. "It's

Kennedy. She came," Diamond said smiling. *Please God, let Blair show up too,* she prayed to herself.

As if the angels heard her pleas, a few minutes later a chauffeur-driven, black tinted Rolls Royce Phantom pulled up.

"Mommy, mommy, Auntie Blair is here!" Elijah exclaimed when she stepped out the car. "Do you think Donovan came?"

"I don't think so, sweetie." Diamond smiled, patting her son's head.

"I still can't believe she went back to that dude," Cameron shook his head and said as Blair and Skee Patron arrived hand in hand.

"All that matters is that she showed up... both of them," Diamond said, thrilled to see her best friends.

It had been a year since Diamond had spoken to Blair or Kennedy. Never did she imagine their reunion would take place at a funeral. Life had torn them apart, it seemed it took death to bring them back together.

18 Months Earlier...

"Get over here, Elijah!" Diamond yelled to her son who was running towards the swings. "Look at him trying to catch up to Donovan." She shook her head.

"Girl, you stay here. I'll go get Elijah. I'm wearing sneakers, you got on those high ass boots which aren't meant for running," Blair cracked.

"I know how to run in heels!" Diamond called out, trailing behind Blair who was already at the swings pushing both boys.

"I told you I had this," Blair said, smiling at Diamond who joined in and started pushing Elijah. His little legs dangled in his seat.

"And let you guys have all the fun?" Diamond laughed. "But I ain't gonna lie. I'm tempted to kick these damn boots off. They definitely ain't meant to be worn at the park."

"True, but you get a pass," Blair said glancing over at Diamond as both women continued to push their giggling sons on the swings while they had girl talk. "It's not like you knew I was going to call and tell you to meet me at Central Park."

"You didn't leave me much of a choice. I mean, I love when we can have these play dates with the kids, but I'm a tad bit overdressed for the occasion," Diamond commented, glancing down at her fitted black pants and silk blouse. "But you said it was urgent and you are my best friend," she said grinning.

"And I do appreciate it."

"So, what's going on? You sounded agitated on the phone."

"Have you spoken to Kennedy?"

"Not in a couple of days. I actually called her this morning, but she didn't answer. Kennedy is on west coast time though, but she still hasn't called me back. She's okay, right?" Diamond questioned becoming worried.

"No, she's fine. I spoke to her right before calling you." Blair let out a deep sigh. "Something seems really off with her."

"Off how?"

"Remember I told you about this major part in that movie I was auditioning for."

"Yeah, you said you thought it went great."

"It did. Kennedy even told me she talked to the producer and it sounded as if I had gotten the role. Did she mention it to you?"

"No. After we stopped being business partners, Kennedy didn't really discuss things like that with me anymore. With her being based in LA and me taking care of a six-year-old and a two-year-old, it doesn't leave much time for those sort of conversations," Diamond said shrugging.

"Well, clearly I was wrong because Kennedy called me today and said I didn't get the part."

"I'm so sorry, Blair. I know how excited you were, but there'll be other auditions."

"I flew to LA three different times to get that role. Kirk was furious because he said it was ridiculous for me to keep dragging our son cross country for a part in a movie that I might not even get." Blair was shaking her head with frustration. "But I knew this was the breakout role that I needed to put me on the map. The director seemed to love me. I don't understand what went wrong."

"Blair, I'm not in the movie business, but things like this can happen. Don't be so hard on yourself."

"I've been in this game long enough to know that sometimes with movies the director might decide to go in a different direction, but I don't get that feeling when it comes to this film. I feel like there is something more…. something doesn't feel right. Like maybe…" Blair's voice trailed off without finishing her sentence.

"Maybe what?" Diamond wanted her friend to finish her thought.

"Maybe Kennedy knows something more than what she's telling me."

Diamond raised her eyebrow not sure what exactly Blair was getting at. "Like Kennedy didn't tell you the real reason you didn't get the part because she didn't want to hurt your feelings or something? Because I seriously doubt that. You know Kennedy is a straight shooter. She's gonna keep it all the way real, good or bad."

"I don't think it's anything like that. When I spoke to her on the phone, I got the feeling she didn't want me to get the part," Blair said frowning.

"Girl, you reaching. You're Kennedy's client. When you win, she wins. That makes no sense."

"On the surface, you're right, but when Kennedy called me with the news, she didn't seem like herself. Normally she would be trying to devise a plan to change the director's mind. Instead she told me about some bullshit modeling gig she got for me."

"I get you're disappointed, Blair. But it sounds like Kennedy is just trying to line up other jobs for you until she can land something bigger."

"Maybe you're right, but I'm sick of modeling. It's so meaningless," Blair spit with irritation. "I'm an actress. I want to focus my career in that direction. If I must be half-naked, I rather it be for a major movie role instead of some dumb photo spread."

"I get your frustration, Blair... I really do. I know your dream has always been to be an actress and you hoped the modeling would lead into that."

"And it did, but then I got pregnant with Donovan. Motherhood became my focus. When I was ready to get back to work, the modeling jobs Kennedy lined up for me were great. It got my name and face back out there so when I got the opportunity for this audition, I put my heart and soul into it. Now I feel like I'm back to square one." Blair's disappointment was plastered across her face.

"Baby girl, you know what they say. It's not about the setback, but the comeback. You got this, Blair. I know you're sick of these modeling gigs, but take them. Trust me, something will lead to another major audition and you'll get the part. You'll be a Hollywood leading lady before you know it." Diamond winked with confidence.

"Daddy, you're home!" Donovan ran to Kirk as his strong arms lifted him up. He tossed his son up in the air a few times before putting him down.

"How my lil' man doing?"

"Good. I went to the park and played on the swings with Elijah," Donovan said.

"Sounds like fun. Go upstairs and check your room. I got a surprise for you," Kirk said grinning. Before he could say another word, Donovan took off running.

"Slow down! Walk, don't run," Blair yelled out, but Donovan was long gone. "So, what's the surprise?"

"That car and racetrack he was begging me for."

"Nice. He probably won't come out his room for the rest of the day," Blair said laughing. "I wasn't expecting you home so soon."

"We got outta practice early today. Maybe we need to take advantage of Donovan being occupied for at least the next hour," Kirk suggested, pulling Blair from behind by the waist.

"Slow down," Blair said giggling as Kirk began sucking down on her neck. "I have a ton of things I need to take care of, but I promise to make it up to you tonight."

"You better." Kirk kept kissing on Blair's neck

while fondling her breasts. "Tonight, can't get here fast enough," he said releasing her from his grasp. "What you wearing to that party tomorrow night?" he questioned casually grabbing a fitness magazine before sitting down on the couch.

"What party?"

"Blair, you can't be serious," he said glancing up for a second before continuing to flip through the magazine. "The GQ party. Remember I told you they want me to do the cover for an upcoming issue."

"That's right, how could I forget. I guess I better find myself something to wear. I'll add that to my to do list for the day."

"Wear something really sexy."

"Whatever you like." Blair smiled, as an idea began spinning in her head. *Maybe I've been going about this all wrong and it's time I take it back to the basics. I'm sure there is going to be a shit load of press there. Instead of worrying about the next gig Kennedy can line up for me, I need to make that red carpet my audition stage. Like she said, you're always on the clock and a photo op leads to more press,* Blair thought to herself. *Yep, Kirk, tomorrow night I'll definitely be wearing something really sexy.*

Chapter Two

Secrets

"I still can't believe they reneged on that part for Blair. We thought for sure she was a shoo-in," Tammy commented to Kennedy when she went into her office to give her some files.

"Yes, it's very disappointing, but we can't worry about that. I have to focus on getting her something else... something better." Kennedy exhaled.

"Do you have any ideas?" Tammy inquired.

"Not at the moment." Kennedy sighed.

"What about that new series on Fox? They're always looking for guest appearances. I know it's not a movie, but it will definitely give Blair some exposure."

"Look into that for me. See who the casting director is. At this point I need to bring something to Blair. She played it cool, but I know she was devastated about not getting that role."

"I'm sure she was. I was devastated for her. No one still hasn't told you why the sudden change?" Tammy asked.

"Nope... but listen, I need to make a few phone calls. Get that information about the casting director for that Fox show."

"I'm on it," Tammy said closing the door on her way out.

Once Kennedy was alone she leaned back in her chair trying to figure out her next move. Only a couple of years ago business was booming and she seemed to be the go to girl for all your publicity needs. Kennedy was also getting more management opportunities based on her success with breaking Blair into the entertainment industry. Then there was one setback after another. Diamond was put on bed rest due to a high-risk pregnancy. Cameron demanded she cut ties with their business because he didn't want her dealing with any unnecessary stress. Kennedy couldn't blame him wanting to protect his wife and unborn child, but it did put the pressure of running a new company squarely on her shoulders. Then the major shift on how to get your voice heard didn't help Kennedy's cause. With the huge free platform of social media, artists no longer felt it necessary to shell out thousands of dollars for a publicist unless it was for major damage control.

On top of that, it became almost impossible to reel in new clients to manage once Blair fell off the radar due to her pregnancy and being a full-time mom. Even after she said she was ready to get back to work, she was constantly backing out of auditions saying they conflicted with her mommy duties. Then when she finally got Blair the big break she needed to get back in the game, everything just went to shambles and exploded right in her face.

Now Kennedy was left scrambling, trying to figure out how to make everything right. For the first time, she couldn't even come up with one bright idea. Although she wouldn't admit it to anyone, Kennedy was scared.

"Baby, where are you going? Our dinner reservation is at seven and you're not even dressed," Diamond said to Cameron before he had a chance to walk out the door.

"Oh damn! I totally forgot about that. But umm, we can't go. Let's reschedule for tomorrow night."

"This place stays booked. It's the hottest new restaurant in the city. It took me forever to get this reservation."

"When you call to cancel, put the reservation in my name. Then you won't have any problems."

"Why do we need to cancel when we can go tonight?"

"Babe, coach called an emergency meeting tonight. I'm on my way there now. It sounds serious so I know I'ma be there for a while. "I'm sorry, but I promise to make it up to you," Cameron said giving Diamond a quick kiss on the lips before heading out.

Diamond let out a disappointing sigh and slumped down on the couch. She was tempted to go take a shower and forget about Cameron ruining their dinner plans, but she couldn't shake this nagging feeling in her stomach. Diamond got up and placed a call.

"Hey girl, I was just thinking about you," Blair said when she answered.

"Foreal! Why was I on your mind?"

"Well, you are my bestie so you're always on my mind in some capacity."

"How sweet," Diamond said smiling.

"Yeah... yeah, but I was wondering if you and Cameron were coming to that GQ party tomorrow night."

"He hasn't mentioned it to me."

"Well Kirk is more of the party scene type. I was hoping you all were coming so you could keep me company, but I'll be fine."

"Yeah, the party scene isn't really Cameron's

thing. Are you and Kirk getting out tonight?" Diamond questioned. Trying to get some information out of Blair without being obvious.

"Nope. I still have to figure out what I'm wearing to this GQ event and Kirk just got home. He said he's in for the night. What about you and Cameron... wait, weren't you all supposed to be going to that new restaurant tonight?" Blair remembered Diamond mentioning it earlier.

"Oh, yeah we decided to wait and go tomorrow night instead."

"I guess that means you definitely won't be coming to this GQ event. Honestly, I wish we were having dinner with the two of you instead."

"Why don't you?"

"Kirk is supposed to be doing a cover for GQ so he really wants to attend this event. I'm also hoping to work some magic there, but we can discuss that later because Kirk just walked in the room," Blair whispered.

"Go 'head and tend to Kirk and we'll catch up later," Diamond said.

"Cool!"

Diamond kept her composure while talking to Blair, but she was ready to smash out a window. *I knew he was lying!* Diamond thought after hanging up. *How the fuck do you and Kirk play for the same damn team, but he's chillin' at home and yo' ass at a damn team meeting. All lies!*

Diamond picked the phone back up and started to dial Cameron's number, but immediately hung up. She decided calling and cursing him the hell out while being so upset was the wrong move.

"What the fuck is really going on with you, Cameron," she seethed talking to herself out loud. "There's only one way to find out."

Chapter Three

Fading Into Oblivion

Blair stood in front of the 43x79 inch mirror, still indecisive about what she was wearing, with less than an hour before it was time for them to leave. What started with five choices was now down to two.

"Should I wear the Marchesa or the Reem Acra?" Blair questioned holding each dress against her naked body.

"Hope you almost ready!" she heard Kirk knock on the door and say.

"Just about!" Blair yelled out, not completely lying. Her hair and makeup was already done so now it came down to her attire. "You gotta get it right," Blair mumbled.

This wasn't just a regular red carpet she was walking as Kirk's date. Blair was hoping to reignite her career. She wasn't sure when she would have another opportunity to shine on such a large platform and needed to take full advantage.

"Come on, Blair, it's time to go." Blair glanced over at the clock and realized twenty minutes had already passed. "We're already running late," Kirk said, pounding on the door.

Blair made what she considered a pivotal decision and went with the Marchesa.

"I swear I shoulda never let you turn that bedroom into a closet. You spend more time in there than the fuckin' bedroom," Kirk huffed.

"Can you blame me," she said giggling, putting on her shoes hurriedly while coming out the door. As a Christmas gift Kirk let Blair turn one of the guest bedrooms into a luxury walk-in closet. The mirrored furniture and shelf details together with the dim lights made it one of the most elegant closets anyone had ever seen. When Blair sat down in her extremely feminine and highly sophisticated satin chair admiring her designer clothes, bags, and shoes, she felt like a princess.

"Nah, I can't blame you. I blame my damn self for paying for that shit," Kirk said shaking his head. "But the way you look in that dress, I guess it was worth it." He grinned giving Blair a kiss.

"I'm glad you approve." Blair took Kirk's hand as they headed out.

"How did the team meeting go yesterday?" Diamond asked casually, taking a sip of her champagne.

"Everything went cool," Cameron answered before biting down on his steak.

"So, what was the emergency?"

"Oh... umm, coach is thinking about making some changes with the lineup and wanted my input."

"What did Kirk and the other players think about the changes the coach wants to make?"

"Kirk wasn't able to make the meeting, but the other players are cool with it. So, how's your food? You've been dying to come to this restaurant and you've barely touched anything on your plate."

"The food is delicious. This champagne just taste a tad bit bitter," she replied coyly. Diamond didn't know if she should be relieved or concerned Cameron willingly acknowledged that Kirk wasn't at yesterday's meeting. Either he was telling the truth and there was a team meeting or he was slick enough to cover his tracks, knowing all Diamond had to do was place a call to her best friend and find out Kirk's whereabouts.

Although she wanted to press a bit more, Diamond decided to ease up on her interrogation. In case he was lying, she didn't want to alert Cameron of her suspicions. Because if he was doing some foul shit, Diamond wanted her husband to feel at ease to carry on, so she could bust his ass.

"Kirk actually asked me stop by this GQ party he was attending tonight," Cameron said glancing down at his watch. "It's still going on now. Do you feel like stopping through after we finish eating?"

"Yeah, Blair did mention us coming to that event, but I told her we had dinner plans. It'll be nice for all of us to hang out together. We haven't done that in a while," Diamond said smiling.

"Yeah, that would be nice." He nodded his head. "So, put the glass down and get to eatin'," Cameron said laughing.

Just like that Diamond threw her misgivings about her husband out the window. *I need to stop worrying so much. Cameron loves me. We have a beautiful family. Our life together is perfect,* she thought looking forward to spending the rest of her evening with her husband and bestie Blair.

Blair did everything but break out into a two-step when she hit the red carpet with Kirk. At first, she played the demure role and was the perfect arm candy for her man. But the instant a photographer who remembered her from her days of being in the spotlight with Skee Patron, recognized her and asked for some solo photo ops, Blair more than willingly obliged. Of course, when one photographer takes interest, the rest fall in line not wanting to miss a so-called opportunity. They figured the person must be important even if they don't know who the fuck they are. Blair took full advantage and was thrilled she chose to wear the mid-length, nude, desire me dress with lace detail and spaghetti straps.

Kirk watched from a short distance with satisfaction mixed with dismay at Blair. He felt proud to have this incredibly sexy woman representing him, but at the same time, she was the mother of his son and all the attention she was garnering had him feeling some type of way.

"You seemed awfully comfortable out there," Kirk commented when Blair finally made her way off her self-made runway. "I was beginning to think you forgot you came with me."

"You're so silly," Blair said giggling, trying to play off just how right Kirk was. She had become a little beside herself. For a moment, she was so caught up in the lights and cameras that she had forgotten she was Kirk's date, until she eyed him standing off to the side. "I was just surprised anyone wanted to take my picture," she lied and said knowing damn well she squeezed into that jaw-dropping dress for that very purpose.

"I hear you," Kirk said taking Blair's hand as they walked into the venue. Once inside, Blair felt that once again she had become invisible. She went from being in the spotlight to just Kirk's date and Blair didn't like it one bit.

"Mr. McKnight, this is your table. Please let me know if you need anything," the hostess assigned to Kirk's table said.

"Thank you." He nodded sitting down. "We have plenty of champagne so we should be good. "Here let me pour you a glass," he said to Blair after the hostess left.

"Thanks. You're not going to pour yourself a glass?"

"In a minute. I need to walk around and speak to a few people."

"Do you want me to come with you?" Blair started to get up.

"No, I'm good. Need to do a lil' politicking. You stay here. I shouldn't be gone long."

Blair slumped back down in her seat folding her arms. This wasn't going the way she visualized. For some reason, she thought if she killed the red carpet outside all that much-needed attention would somehow follow her inside, but nobody gave a damn about her. She was just another pretty girl in a room full of them.

It had been so long since Blair was out at a major event. She had become a full-time soccer mom, without living in the suburbs, but instead in glamorous New York City. Being on the party scene made her realize just how much she hated being a nobody. A few short years ago she was a sought after model/actress who was being labeled the next big thing. Now she had become the invisible girlfriend/baby mother of a superstar NBA player and that was one position Blair had no interest in playing.

"Are you there!" The loud voice shook Blair out of her thoughts.

"Ohmigosh! Diamond, what are you doing here?" Blair stood up with excitement. "I'm so happy to see you!" she said giving her a hug.

"I'm glad to see you too. Whatever you were thinking about had you stuck because I was standing here for a few seconds."

"Sorry about that," Blair said as the ladies sat down. "Did you come by yourself?"

"Of course not," Diamond said laughing. "I came with Cameron. Our dinner ended early and he suggested we come here. I was thrilled because I knew I would see you."

"So, where's Cameron?"

"Walking around. I saw you and he knew I would much rather be over here than walking around while he talked to random people I didn't know. Where's Kirk?"

"He's walking around too. Unlike you though, I would like to be walking around with him, but he wanted me to stay seated over here like a good puppy." Blair frowned pouring herself another glass of champagne then filling up a glass for Diamond too.

"Blair, don't say it like that. I'm sure Kirk figured you would be comfortable chillin' over here."

"Why would he think that? Because I should be satisfied being the girlfriend of Kirk McKnight since that's such an important title to have?" Blair stated sarcastically rolling her eyes.

"That's not what I'm saying."

"Then what are you saying, Diamond? I mean seriously, don't you ever get tired of being known as Cameron Robinson's wife? You were Miss Independent and now your identity comes from being an NBA wife. That doesn't annoy you even a little bit?"

Diamond paused for a minute, took a sip of her champagne and shrugged her shoulders. "Nope, not at all. I love being a wife and mother. I have the life that most women dream of."

"Not this woman. My greatest ambition in life isn't being married to some athlete," she huffed, leaning back in her seat. "No offense, Diamond."

"No offense taken. But I thought you were loving being a stay-at-home mom?"

"I did, but now Donovan goes to preschool and we have a great nanny so that I have some free time to go on auditions. But nothing is happening for me. I thought that movie role would finally give me back my own identity, but now I'm right back in the same position. I'm sick of this shit. If something doesn't pop soon, I might have to turn into one of those Instagram models that host bullshit parties for a living."

Blair and Diamond both burst out laughing. "Girl, don't you dare!" Diamond giggled loudly.

"I'm not that desperate, but I'm getting close. I thought coming to this party would create all these opportunities for me and put me back on the path to success, but it was nothing but a waste of my fuckin' time. Something has to give because I refuse to let a once-promising career fade into oblivion," Blair made clear.

Chapter Four

In My Feelings

"Diamond, this is a pleasant surprise. How are you?"

Kennedy said pulling into the parking lot at her office building.

"I'm doing great. I know I should call more often, but between being a wife and mommy duties, there never seems to be enough time. Right before I called you, I realized I never got back to you after you left me those messages. I'm so sorry. Please forgive me. Is everything okay?"

"No apology necessary. I know you're busy."

"But you should always make time for a friend. Honestly, it slipped my mind. Between keeping up with Destiny and Elijah I barely remember my own name. I might need to do like Blair and get a nanny," Diamond said laughing.

"Diamond, it's really okay," Kennedy insisted.

"Thanks for being so understanding. Enough about me how is everything going with you and the business?"

"I'm doing great and business is awesome," Kennedy lied.

"Why am I not surprised... you're like super-woman."

"That's me, the lady who wears a cape with the letter S on it," Kennedy joked, although she wanted to pull her hair out from the stress of trying to get her business back on track.

"You're so silly, Kennedy! I can always count on you to make me laugh. But turning things a little more serious, I wanted to speak to you about Blair."

"What about her?"

"I saw her a few nights ago and she's really taking losing out on that movie role really hard."

"I know and I really feel bad about that, but that's how business goes sometimes. A role is never guaranteed until you're in front of the camera and you shoot your part. Even then it might end up on the cutting room floor."

"I get that and so does Blair, but she really believed that part was hers. Now that she didn't get the role, she's starting to feel like her time is up and she won't be getting any more opportunities."

"I'm constantly presenting Blair with opportunities, but she always turns them down. She thinks they're beneath her."

"Well, after the success she had in the past you can understand her not wanting to do low level gigs."

"The key word is past. In this industry, you're only as good as your last part and Blair hasn't had one in a few years. That's ancient in this business. Nobody told Blair to go have a baby and become a stay-at-home mom."

"I get that, but..."

"But nothing!" Kennedy snapped, interrupting Diamond. "She's basically a newbie again in this industry and that means she has to start from the bottom and try to work her way back up. So, at this point no gig I present is beneath her or low level," she snarled. She took a huge gulp of her Espresso Macchiato hoping the caffeine rush would instantly kick in as she sat in her car talking to Diamond.

"Kennedy, I wasn't trying to offend you. I know you are doing everything possible to jumpstart Blair's career and if you could've sealed the deal on her movie role, you would have. I'm just really concerned about Blair. I remember how insecure Michael made her feel because she completely relied on him for everything. Although Kirk isn't an asshole like Michael was, I can tell that Blair is starting to question her worth because she's now solely relying on Kirk. I just want her to feel independent again. That's when she was the happiest I've ever seen her."

"Trust me, I get what you're saying. Nothing is more empowering than knowing you can make it on your own. I promise you, I'm doing everything possible to make Blair into a star."

I need for that to happen more than you know or I'll be shutting down my business and be on the unemployment line, Kennedy thought to herself.

"Have you received your first payment from Kennedy yet? Of course not!" Darcy laughed hysterically while lying in bed next to Michael.

"She still has time so don't get excited just yet."

"Oh, please. Kennedy won't come up with the money." Darcy smiled in delight. "Boy, oh boy I can't wait for her to default on her loan so I can tell her that I'm the owner of her company."

"You mean co-owner being that I have the majority percentage."

"I know that, Michael, but you won't be the one running the day-to-day operation. That will be me. Besides, by the time we take over, I'll have to rebuild her business from scratch because I doubt she'll have any clients left."

"I could care less what you do with that business. There's only one client I have an interest in."

"Of course... Blair," Darcy said sighing. "She's the only reason you agreed to give me the money so I could execute my sweet revenge on Kennedy."

"I'll admit you've always been a pro schemer. But when you told me this particular scheme would keep Blair from securing a movie role she desperately wanted, that was all I needed to hear."

"I know. That's why I brought my proposal to you. I knew you would jump at the opportunity to get back at your ex. After all this time, you're not over the fact that she left you." Darcy shook her head angrily. She was full of rage and jealousy that Michael was still carrying a torch for Blair. She never wanted to admit that she was the other woman like Kennedy said, but Darcy could no longer deny the truth and it was eating her up.

"Blair gave up her life with me to be some baby mother to a dumb athlete," Michael scoffed, stepping out the bed.

"The audacity!" Darcy exclaimed. "What was she thinking?"

"Exactly! Clearly she wasn't." Michael's arrogance and ego was so out of control, he had no clue that Darcy was being cynical with her comment so he continued on. "Blair has never been the brightest light in the harbor and leaving me for that loser Kirk proves that."

"You're absolutely right, but her loss is my gain." Darcy rose in the bed and reached over to Michael's naked body trying to pull him back in the bed. Darcy knew that Michael was a self-absorbed asshole, but every time she saw his succulent, sculpted body, she became weak. That was no easy feat for an ice queen like Darcy.

"Not right now." Michael shrugged her off.

"Come on. I know how to make you feel better," Darcy teased, fixing her eyes on Michael's well-endowed manhood.

"I guess you can suck on it for a little while," Michael told Darcy like he was doing her a favor and her mouth wasn't about to be putting in all the work.

"Thank you, baby." Darcy smiled before opening wide and taking all of him inside her wet mouth.

Chapter Five

Don't Go

Blair was leaving her kickboxing class listening to Kehlani when she noticed Kennedy was calling. Initially she let it go to voicemail preferring to listen to the melodic sounds coming from her headphones instead of getting into yet another heated conversation with Kennedy. Lately they couldn't seem to agree on anything including what direction to take her career. After the third time of her calling back, Blair finally decided to answer.

"Hey!" Blair did her best to sound upbeat.

"Didn't you see me calling you?" Kennedy's accusatory attitude wasn't helping Blair to maintain her fake bubbly persona, but she pressed on.

"I was in kickboxing class and just saw I missed your call," she replied, sticking to a half lie.

"Oh, well that's an acceptable reason to miss my calls. It's important you keep that body in prime condition."

"True indeed... so what's going on."

"I have something lined up for you," Kennedy said in an almost singing tone.

"Kennedy, I already told you I'm not being the model for a relaxer box. I don't care how many times you ask or what perks the company throws in. Besides I'm natural anyway." Blair was already regretting she answered Kennedy's call.

"Although I still believe doing that campaign as their spokesmodel would've garnered you a ton of exposure, it's a new day and we don't need that shit anymore," Kennedy stated proudly.

"Really?! So, you weren't blowing up my phone to try and convince me for the hundredth time to take that gig?"

"Nope!"

"Then what do you have lined up for me?"

"This is major! No, it's not a movie role, but it's great money and the exposure will be amazing for your career."

"Tell me! Tell me!" Blair blurted out eager to find out what Kennedy had lined up.

"Apple wants you to be the leading lady for their new campaign. As of now you will be in at least three national and international commercials."

"Wait, do you mean the Apple that makes the iPhone I'm talking to you on right now?"

"Yep, the one and only."

"Get the FUCK outta here!" Blair started jumping up and down hysterically in the middle of a busy New York City block. She then calmed herself down needing further confirmation before she continued on like a crazy person. "Do I actually have the part or am I being considered and need to audition?"

"Babygirl, it's yours. Things are moving so fast they already had the contract delivered to my office. It's a done deal once you sign on the dotted line."

"I can't believe this shit. Finally, the break I've been waiting for. Thank you, so, so, so much, Kennedy. I know it's the hard work you've been putting in behind the scenes that made this possible. After that movie role fell through, I doubted there was a place left for me in this industry, but you came through and saved the day. Thank you!"

"Before you thank me, there is one thing you have to do."

"What's that?"

"Be on a flight tomorrow morning to LA. They're already behind schedule and need to start filming the commercial ASAP," Kennedy informed Blair.

"I'll be there," Blair stated adamantly. "I'm not

letting another opportunity slip through my fingers."

"That's my girl! I'll send you over your flight information. See you in LA!" Kennedy beamed before ending their call.

Blair continued doing the happy dance as she celebrated the wonderful news all the way home. When she walked through the front door, the jubilation was still written all over her face.

"Damn, what has you in such a good mood?" Kirk commented when Blair twirled into the bedroom.

"Kennedy finally came through and got me a major commercial with Apple!"

"Apple as in iPhone Apple?" Kirk questioned as in disbelief.

"OMG! That's the same thing I asked Kennedy when she told me about it. Yes! That fuckin' Apple. How incredible is that!"

"Wow, that's what's up."

"I know. Everything is moving so fast, but in a good way. I have to be in LA tomorrow because they want to start shooting the commercial immediately, so I need to pack."

"Wait, you're leaving for LA tomorrow... what about Donovan?" Kirk questioned.

"I already spoke to Jillian and she'll be able to stay here and take care of Donovan while I'm gone. You know how great she is with him so they'll be fine."

"How long will you be gone?"

"I'm not sure. Kennedy didn't say, but it shouldn't be more than a week."

"A week to film a fuckin' commercial?"

"Kirk, I said no longer than a week. It might only be a couple days. Kennedy didn't have a lot of details for me, but once I get to LA I'll have a better idea." Blair sighed heading to her closet so she could start packing.

"Are you sure you even got the part? I would hate for you to fly all the way to LA and find out you no longer have the part," he remarked.

"I'm sure you're referring to me being dropped from that movie, but no worries, Kennedy said the contract has already been delivered to her office. But I appreciate your concern." Blair glared at Kirk.

"I don't think you should be away from Donovan for that long. He needs his mother."

"He needs his father too and when you're out on the road for weeks at a time, I make sure to hold it down. Like I said, Jillian has me covered until I get back. That's why we hired a nanny in the first place, for situations like this."

"When I'm out on the road, it's so I can afford to pay for shit like this fuckin' expensive ass closet you like to parade around in. And this luxury crib you wanna lounge in... let's not forget those expensive whips you drive around in. So don't compare me being on the road to collect my NBA checks to you doing some fuckin' commercial," Kirk scoffed.

"This commercial could lead to a lot more opportunities for me."

"Opportunities for what? Huh? I don't care how many commercials or movie roles you get, it won't be able to afford you this," he said putting his hand up as if capturing all of the opulence. "You need to forget about these Hollywood dreams. You're a mother now. I told you I was ready for us to get married. You should be focused on planning a wedding not catching a flight to LA."

"Married! You cheated on me less than six months ago."

"I was on the road and made a mistake. I thought we had put that behind us."

"Yes, we're trying to make our relationship work, but we're not ready for marriage. I still don't trust you. I can't marry a man I don't trust."

"Us being apart isn't going to help to rebuild that trust," Kirk shot back.

"I'm not gonna be gone that long, Kirk," Blair snapped becoming frustrated with his attitude. "Please don't fight me on this. You know I want a career. I'll probably never get another chance like this again. Can you just be supportive?"

"Blair, I love you and I want you to be my wife. I still have the ring," he reached out taking her hand. "I'm just waiting for you to put it on. Don't go chasing Hollywood dreams, when you have everything you need standing right here in front of you to make them come true." Kirk said his peace and walked away leaving Blair alone to marinate on his words.

There was no doubt that Blair loved Kirk very much, but not enough to cease her desire for stardom.

Chapter Six

Hold On You

"Whatever you're looking at on your phone must be good because I haven't seen you smile like that in weeks," Sebastian commented, walking into the kitchen.

"Blair sent me a text saying her flight just arrived, so yes I'm ecstatic. I wasn't sure she would make it."

"This is a major commercial. I'm sure she wouldn't miss that flight," he said opening the refrigerator and taking out some orange juice.

"Blair always has the best intentions, but things can go either way when it comes to her. Plus, I'm sure Kirk wasn't thrilled she was leaving."

"He isn't supportive of her career?"

"It's crazy because when she initially met Kirk, he was super supportive. But after Donovan was born and them eventually working things out and moving in together, pursuing movie roles is the last thing he wants her to do."

"There goes that frown again," Sebastian cracked.

"Is it that obvious," Kennedy sighed. "I finally have a chance to get Blair's career poppin' and I don't need Kirk whispering in her ear trying to shut it down. Blair getting this gig is the best news I've gotten in a while. I don't need anything or anyone messing this up."

"Kennedy, you sound stressed. I know you mentioned business was a little slow, but are things worse than what you told me?"

"It's nothing I can't handle," she remarked sounding defensive.

"You know you can come to me if you need help."

"I appreciate that, but like I said, it's handled. I have to go," Kennedy said grabbing her purse and some papers off the counter. "I'm meeting Blair at her hotel before heading over to the location where they're shooting the commercial. I'll call you later."

Kennedy could see the concern on Sebastian's face, but she refused to acknowledge it. To admit that she had needed his help would've made her feel like a failure. That's why instead of turning to her man when her business was crumbling, she made a deal with someone who would help her cause, or so Kennedy thought.

"Coach worked the fuck outta us today," Cameron said slamming his locker closed.

"You ain't lying. We ain't practiced that hard in a minute. I guess we needed it." Kirk laughed, thinking how the whole team had been slacking lately.

"You up for blowing off a lil' steam now that we done put that work in."

"What you go in mind?" Kirk inquired.

"Hittin' up this party."

"In the middle of the afternoon?" Kirk chuckled.

"Man, this party be lit all day. So, you in?" Cameron questioned.

Cameron had peaked his interest. Kirk wondered what sort of party could be lit at this time of the day... none that he had been to. Plus, he needed something to get his mind off Blair. He didn't like how they left things before she went out of town and he honestly was tired of thinking about it.

"Yeah, I'm in. Let's go.

When Cameron and Kirk arrived at brownstone in Harlem, the first thing Kirk noticed was all the luxury cars lining the street. Cameron headed towards the front door with purpose in every step, he almost seemed on a mission. Kirk was right behind him as if he would be left outside if he didn't keep up.

"What up, Cam!" the big burly man said as if he and Cameron were the best of friends. "You got here right on time. They 'bout to start."

"Perfect!" Cameron had this twinkle in his eyes and hurried downstairs. The big burly man nodded at Kirk as he hurried to catch up with Cameron. Kirk noticed the man was carrying heat. He made a quick notation and kept it moving.

"Damn man, can you slow down!" Kirk called out. He figured whatever was about to start up had to be hella fire.

Besides all the designer whips outside nothing was giving Kirk a lit party until they entered through the third set of doors. *I Run New York* was the first sound they heard blasting through the speakers. The "I Get Money" remix with 50 Cent, Diddy, and Jay Z was blaring. You couldn't help but get hyped hearing the throwback head banger. There was a DJ, cocktail waitresses that were scantily dressed in a classy way, if that was possible, a full bar, plush couches, and even a dance floor. But Cameron bypassed all that. He came for one reason, the poker table.

Kirk watched as his friend and teammate sat down at the round table that already had five other men seated. He noticed one of the men was a player from the opposing team they were playing tomorrow. The other men just looked like rich street niggas. Kirk took a seat on the couch where there was a small crowd surrounding the table. He saw Cameron pull out a shit load of Benjamins.

Yo, this nigga playin' wit' real money, Kirk thought to himself. *That's why they got that big mutherfucka up there wit' that gun.* Knowing the stakes were high put a certain thrill to the situation. Kirk called over the waitress to order a drink. He decided he might as well get comfortable and enjoy the show.

"Are you sure you don't want me to stay here with you? I really don't mind?" Kennedy said to Blair when they pulled up to the studio where the commercial was being filmed.

"Kennedy, I'll be fine. I know this is Apple, but it isn't my first commercial," Blair said smiling. "Plus, I don't want anyone thinking I need someone to hold my hand."

"A lot of talent have their publicist and managers with them. I just so happen to be both for you," Kennedy cracked.

"I know and you're absolutely right, but I want to set the tone as being more laidback. The paperwork has been signed. Everything is a go so we're good."

"I get it! My Blair is growing up. You're not the nervous Nancy you used to be," Kennedy joked. "Well my office isn't far from here so if you need me, I'm just a phone call away."

"Thanks, love," Blair said leaning over and giving Kennedy a hug. "If I'm not too tired after we finish filming maybe we can go out for a drink."

"Sounds like a plan. Talk to you later." Kennedy watched Blair head inside and she felt proud to see her so confident and self assured. There was a time Kennedy questioned if Blair would ever get to a point in her life that she would feel strong enough to stand on her own. She finally seemed to be on a path to do just that.

"You must be Blair," the petite lady greeted Blair and said.

"Yes," she replied with a wide smile.

"I'm Leslie. They're waiting for you in hair and makeup. Follow me. Feel free to get yourself something to eat or drink," she commented as Blair glanced over at the array of food set up buffet-style.

"I'm good. I'll just have some water," she said snatching up a bottle of Fiji before sitting down.

Wasting not a second, the makeup artist went in on Blair's face like she was on the clock and time was running out. It seemed like within a flash she was done and out the makeup chair and on to hair. It all went so fast, Blair was concerned that her face wasn't beat properly. But she was pleasantly surprised when she saw that her face was flawless.

"Wow, she did an amazing job," Blair stated out loud.

"You sound surprised," Maurice, the guy doing her hair remarked.

"She did it so fast. I guess I wasn't expecting this sort of result."

"I know what you mean. Everyone says that, but Kirsten is the ultimate pro. She's been doing it so long that I believe she could slay a face with her eyes closed."

"Wow, that's amazing. I'm lucky to have her and you for that matter," Blair commented noticing how he had her blow out looking like she just left the Dominican salon.

"You know I'ma have you looking like a superstar. Hell, when I'm done with you, they'll think it's your commercial instead of Skee's." Maurice laughed loudly.

"Did you say Skee as in Skee Patron?"

"What other Skee is there?" Maurice raised an

eyebrow as if unsure whether Blair was joking or being serious.

"I mean I knew there was a major music star headlining the commercial, but nobody told me who it was and I didn't ask," Blair admitted.

"I assumed you knew. If my memory serves me right, weren't you two an item at one time? Not trying to be nosy, but I do read the blogs and I remember you and him being posted on them numerous times."

"You're right. We did date, but we haven't been in touch for a very long time."

"Well, I guess you all are about to reunite," Maurice said, turning his head.

Through the mirror, Blair looked to see what had caught Maurice's attention. She then saw Skee coming towards them. "I guess we are about to reunite," Blair mumbled wishing she could stop the butterflies in her stomach. But there was no denying that after all this time, Skee still had a hold on her.

Chapter Seven

Like Old Times

All eyes were on the table waiting anxiously for the next move. Thousands had been lost and then won again which had the crowd on edge.

"I'll buy," a dude named Packer said, holding his cards like he was doing everyone at the table a favor. Cameron shot an intense glare at him and then looked down at his cards. Packer had won the last three rounds so it would seem almost logical for the players to go ahead and fold, but Cameron wasn't having it. He had a feeling that Packer was bluffing with his 'I'll buy the pot' offer.

"Nah, I'm good." Cameron nodded and the other players followed suit.

"Have it yo' way." Packer snarled trying to sound unbothered, but unable to conceal his irritation. "Remember this a no limit bet."

Kirk had damn near finished an entire bottle of liquor watching Cameron, but it only heightened his focus on the game. He leaned in to scrutinize every move the players were making. One by one they started dropping like flies because they chose to fold. Now there were only three.

"I raise," the other player named Armad stated, but instead of backing off, both Packer and Cameron were all in. This was the highest the stakes had been and each man wanted to win. The game had turned into a showdown. The last three remaining players turned their cards over to determine who had the best hand. Armad showed his hand first as if confident he would come out on top. He had four of a kind.

"Not tonight, my nigga," Packer boasted revealing a straight flush. The smile that followed seemed to be shining brighter than the diamonds beaming from his wrist and the pendant on his chain. His hand reached forward to retrieve the stacks and stacks of Benjamins on the table.

"Don't forget about the last dog in this fight." Cameron gave a devilish chuckle before showing the fuck out with a royal flush. Five cards in order. Ace, King, Queen, Jack, and 10, all the same suit.

It felt like the entire room gasped at the same

time. Kirk didn't know much about Poker, but with all those spades on the table, he figured that shit must be good.

"Fuck that shit! You cheated nigga!" Packer jumped up from his chair and barked. Swinging his hat off and throwing it down on the table.

"Cheated wit' what... ghost cards?" Cameron shot back. Everybody started laughing to Packer's disdain.

"He got a point," the dealer added, knowing there was no way possible Cameron could've cheated on his watch. But that didn't deter Packer from having a grown man tantrum.

"Let me collect my winnings so I can go." Cameron said smoothly, gathering up his coins.

"Nah, fuck that! Let's go another round. Right now!" Packer insisted.

"I'm done for today, but I'll be back. But make sure you got yo' money up," Cameron said smirking.

"What the fuck you mean?! You ain't the only nigga in here makin' millions. Don't let those NBA checks go to yo' head... have you fucked up in these streets."

"Is you fuckin' threatening me?" Cameron paused.

"I'm sayin' money and fame got yo' mind twisted. But I deal wit' bigger stars than you so stop feelin' yo'self before you hurt yo'self," Packer said smirking.

"Negro, please," Cameron mocked which pissed Packer off even more.

"Security!" Kirk heard one of the cocktail waitresses yell out.

"Come on, man. Let's go," Kirk said reaching for Cameron's arm. He was already intoxicated and though he felt he could connect on a few punches, Kirk wasn't exactly in the best mindset for a brawl.

"Packer, chill out before you don't get invited back," the dealer warned.

"Whatever! You go 'head and take this chump change. But get ready for that 'L' I got for you," Packer groaned as he and his crew left out.

"Yo, I was gon' ask you to teach me how to play poker, but I'ma dead that shit. Niggas out here ready to catch a charge behind a card game," Kirk huffed shaking his head.

"Man, Packer all bark. Every time he loses he have a meltdown. Only time that nigga happy is when he winning. But he always come back. Maybe this time he'll stay gone," Cameron said. "Come on, let's go eat. Dinner on me."

"Betta be. All that money you just won." Both men laughed as they made their way out the door.

"It's been a long time," Skee stood behind Blair and said.

"Yeah, feels like old times when we first met on the set of your music video."

"Not really. You didn't have a child and you weren't living with another man. How is Donovan doing by the way?"

Blair saw Maurice press his lips together and his eyes widened, but he kept doing her hair as if he didn't catch the shade.

"Donovan is doing fantastic," Blair said not keeping it short.

"I'm glad. I'll let you finish up and I'll see you on set." Skee walked off leaving Blair feeling even more confused by the knots in her stomach.

"Well, well. So that's the notorious Skee Patron. I guess what they say is true," Maurice smacked.

"So, this is your first time working with Skee?"

"Yep."

"So, what exactly did you hear about him?" Blair was curious to know.

"Basically, that he ain't got no filter and he gon' say and do whatever he like. That's just the impression I got from him during that little exchange the two of you just had," he scoffed.

"Yeah, that pretty much sums Skee up," Blair agreed. "I guess you either love him or hate him."

"He's makin' millions... has millions of fans, clearly somebody love him... maybe even you."

"Huh?!" Maurice caught Blair completely off

guard with his comment. Her face frowned up.

"I'm sorry! I didn't mean to offend you," he said shrugging.

"I'm not offended. I just don't know why you would say something like that." Blair found her response full of stutter.

"I don't know. It felt like there is some un-finished business between the two of you... am I wrong?"

"Aren't you bold with your questions. Geesh!"

"I know. That's what everybody say," Maurice admitted with no shame. "When you do as much hair as I do, you can't help but become bold with questions. But I'm pretty good at reading who sittin' in my chair. I can tell who I can be real with and who I need to just do their hair and keep it moving. You feel me." Maurice put his hand on his hip waiting for Blair to respond.

"Yes, I feel you, Maurice, but I think you read me wrong."

"No, the hell I didn't," he said, giggling sarcas-tically. "You just ain't ready to admit the shit. But that's cool. We got three days left on this shoot so we got time," Maurice said smiling.

"Kennedy, I wasn't expecting to hear back from you

so soon. I hope you're not calling to ask for more time. Like I said the last time we talked, I can't extend your time. Friday is the latest I can give you for the first installment of your payment."

"Actually, I was calling to let you know that I'll have the money for you tomorrow," Kennedy informed him.

"Really?" Barry questioned leaning back in his chair.

"Why do you sound so surprised? I thought I would hear an upbeat, happy tone to the news."

"Of course, I'm happy," Barry lied, tossing his pen down on the desk. "Business must be looking up."

"It is... slowly but surely things are looking up. That loan you gave me came with some pretty stiff penalties, but with the way things are going, it was worth it," Kennedy beamed, feeling optimistic for the first time in months.

"Glad to hear it. I'll be looking for the first payment tomorrow and the rest to follow."

"No worries, Barry. I will be paying back every dime I owe you on time," Kennedy promised without hesitation. With the commission she was making off Blair's commercial she had reason to sound confident. She also had some other potential deals lined up that would bring in a nice chunk of change so Kennedy was feeling extra buoyant.

"Thanks for letting me know and I'll talk to

you soon," Barry said hanging up with Kennedy and immediately calling Darcy.

"Good afternoon, Barry. Just the person I was waiting to hear from," Darcy beamed. "I appreciate you calling me first before telling Michael the good news. I guess he wouldn't consider Kennedy defaulting on her loan so soon good news," she continued. Darcy would've continued having a one way conversation with herself until Barry finally shut her up.

"Darcy! Can you please contain yourself and let me talk?" he barked through the phone.

"No need to yell. All you had to do was ask," Darcy said sighing.

"I just got off the phone with Kennedy and she'll have her first payment tomorrow."

"That can't be! How?" Darcy was gripping her phone in disbelief.

"I don't know and I didn't want to ask. She was already questioning why I seemed unenthusiastic about getting some of my money back."

"You mean Michael's money," Darcy snarled.

"You know what I meant," Barry sniped back. "Don't forget you came to me for help."

"That might be true, but don't act like you didn't benefit from this or your client for that matter," Darcy reminded him.

"Listen, I need to get back to work," Barry said, regretting he called Darcy in the first place. "I'll get the money to Michael as soon as Kennedy makes payment."

"But..." before Darcy could get the rest of her words out she realized Barry had hung up on her. "Asshole!" she screamed, slamming her phone down.

Darcy was livid. She was ready to see the demise of Kennedy and preferred it to come sooner rather than later. Darcy went from having a booming business with an office in a New York City high rise to working out of her apartment and she put the blame solely on Kennedy.

After orchestrating the fake baby mama scandal that kept Cameron headlining the gossip blogs, everything went south when Sharon went *loco* and tried to kill Diamond. To make matters worse, Sharon went on a full fledge press tour, taking interviews with anyone who would listen while she was awaiting trial, blaming the entire ordeal on Darcy.

After Sharon took a plea and was sentenced to prison, everyone said that Darcy Woods should be sharing a cell with her. All her clients dropped her and just like that she was no longer the most sought after publicist in the city. When word got back to Darcy that Kennedy was the one making sure Sharon had full access to the media to tell her story, she vowed to destroy her nemesis if it was the last thing she did.

How in the hell did Kennedy come up with the money! Only a miracle could've saved her. I need to find out what she has going on and put a stop to it because that bitch is going down, Darcy swore.

Chapter Eight

Making Demands

"Great job! That's it for today. I'll see all of you back here tomorrow," the producer told everyone on set.

"You've been off the scene for a minute. I was a lil' worried you wouldn't be able to deliver. I'm glad you proved me wrong," Skee said to Blair as she was heading to her dressing room.

"I'm surprised you didn't have me replaced when you found out I had been cast. I'm sure you had the clout to do so."

"You're right, I did, but it's not my style to stop somebody from eatin', even if it is my ex."

"Thank you. I really needed this gig. I appreciate you not stopping it. It's kinda crazy because doing that video with you years ago was my big break and now this commercial will be my big comeback."

"Does that mean you owe me?" Skee questioned.

"That depends."

"Depends on what?"

"What I owe you," Blair said shrugging.

"I'm starving so we can start with dinner."

"I have worked up an appetite... dinner it is," she said smiling.

"Your treat." Skee winked.

"Good choice and the prices aren't bad either," Blair commented scanning through the menu."

"Yeah, 71Above is one of my favorite spots. Not only is the food good, but with it being on top of the US Bank Tower, it has these sweeping views of the entire city in all directions. Can't beat that," Skee said calling over their waitress.

"You know what you're getting already? We just sat down."

"I'm ordering a bottle of bubbly."

"Um, I said I was treating for dinner. A bottle of champagne was not part of the agreement. That's a few hundred dollars right there."

"I'm sure you can afford it wit' those child support checks you cashing."

"Funny." Blair rolled her eyes not amused.

"I was only joking. I know you and Kirk 'bout to walk down the aisle so I'm sure instead of child support checks, he has you on a nice allowance."

"The jokes just keep coming from you tonight."

"My apologies. I do tend to take jokes too far sometimes." Skee noticed the frown on Blair's face and how quick her upbeat attitude disappeared.

"It's not you. I guess I wish what you said was a lie, but the joke is, Kirk does give me an allowance." Blair put her head down as if she was embarrassed to admit that.

"Blair..."

"Please don't give me a fake apology or some bullshit words of encouragement to make me feel better out of guilt."

"I must've really struck a nerve wit' you."

Blair looked away trying to get her thoughts together before answering. But instead of conjuring up what sounded right she kept it real.

"When I said, I needed this gig, it wasn't just so I could get back in the business. It was also because I needed the money. I've been relying on Kirk financially since having our son. At first it didn't bother me because I wanted to be a stay-at-home mom and give him all my attention. But as Donovan got older I started to hate myself and resent Kirk."

"This isn't some bullshit words of encouragement, but you shouldn't be so hard on yourself, Blair.

Although I've never done it," Skee said laughing, "But being a good mother must be one of, if not, the hardest jobs in the world. You deserve to be properly taken care of for being a great mom to Donovan. So, you definitely have no reason to hate yourself."

"Thank you for saying that."

"I'm speaking the truth. It's also true that you should consider yourself lucky for having a child with a man that has the money to provide for you and Donovan properly. So, don't resent Kirk. I'm sure he loves both you deeply."

"Wow, did I just hear you say something nice about Kirk?!" Blair sounded stunned.

"I did have my issues with Kirk, especially how he treated you during and after your pregnancy. But he stepped up and seems to be doing right by you... or is he?" Skee questioned, sensing some unhappiness with Blair.

Blair hesitated. She was about to express her feelings regarding Kirk, but changed her mind. "I don't wanna talk about my relationship with Kirk tonight. I want to have a nice dinner, drink some of that champagne that *you're* buying." She laughed stressing the word 'you're'. "And soak in this amazing LA view."

"Say no more. Let's pop some bottles." Skee reached over and placed his hand on top of Blair's. He missed having her in his life and now that Blair was back, Skee wanted to keep it that way.

"Can you believe how that nigga tried to play me!" Packer barked getting out of bed.

"Babe, that was yesterday. I can't believe you woke up still thinking about that shit." Lyric sighed, pulling the duvet cover over her face, trying to go back to sleep.

"Fuck that and fuck Cameron Robinson! He thinks he hot shit cause he a fuckin' NBA player. That nigga can get it like anybody else."

Lyric tossed and turned in bed realizing Packer woke up in one of his moods so there was no way she would be able to go back to sleep. She was used to her boyfriend overreacting and carrying on about dumb shit, but she just wasn't in the mood for it this morning. "Baby, calm down and come back to bed." Lyric gave it one last try.

"Nah, we going back to the spot today so I can play that nigga again and this time I'ma win. He can't beat me two days straight, ain't no fuckin' way!" Packer growled as he hit the hardwood floor and started doing his morning ritual of pushups.

Packer continued mouthing off loudly. Lyric rolled her eyes letting out a heavy sigh before getting out of bed. She had to walk past him on her way to the bathroom and Lyric couldn't help but to admire his broad shoulders and well defined muscles.

If this nigga wasn't so fine and rich I would leave his irritating ass alone, Lyric thought to herself as she closed the bathroom door. She let the shower jets drench her body reminiscing how she went from an Instagram Thot to the girlfriend of a crazy drug kingpin.

When Lyric began her social media career by posting scantily clad pictures on her Instagram account, her goal was to get chose by a celebrity singer, rapper, or athlete. After hooking up with a few different ones and it going absolutely nowhere she eventually settled for a celebrity drug dealer. Jermaine Burke better known as Packer in the streets, zeroed in on the busty beauty when one of his homeboys was trolling the gram and came across a provocative image she posted. After liking the photo, he then shared it with Packer. It didn't take long for Packer to hit Lyric up on her DM.

Initially, Lyric was giving Packer no play. She had her sights set on more lucrative opportunities that could have her front and center in the limelight. But the more shade she threw Packer's way the more persistent he became. Being a rich hood star, Packer had no need to pursue a woman, they were too busy pursuing him. So, he enjoyed the chase. Eventually all that chasing paid off. But what was supposed to be a few sex sessions for Packer and a chance for Lyric to stack up on some expensive trinkets, had turned into a full-fledged relationship.

"I need you to call up some of your girlfriends and tell them I have a job for them to do!" Packer barged into the bathroom and yelled, disrupting Lyric's thoughts and shower.

"What kind of job?" Lyric casually asked, not really interested in the answer to his question.

"All you need to tell them is they gon' make a few stacks."

"A piece?" Lyric paused mid-wash, anxiously waiting for Packer's reply. She wasn't interested before, but now she was.

"Yep!" he stated reaching for the toothpaste to brush his teeth.

"How many friends you need?"

"Three of yo' baddest friends."

Lyric immediately started pondering which friends she would call. Christmas was about to come early for three lucky chicks, but deciding who they would be was a little difficult. Lyric had way more than three bad bitches to choose from, so she wanted the dough to go to who needed it the most and worked her nerves the least.

"What should I tell them the job will be?" Lyric inquired, as she was mentally going down her list and crossing off names she knew were a no go.

"Don't worry about that. Just bring the girls ASAP," Packer scoffed.

"No problem, but make sure you got my finder's fee ready for me ASAP," Lyric shot back before continuing with her shower, daring Packer to deny her demand, but at the same time wondering what the hell he was up to.

Chapter Nine

Can't Have Everything

"Baby, I was thinking maybe we could have another dinner date night. But this time have the kids spend the night at my mother's house so we can come home and have the place to ourselves." Diamond gave Cameron a seductive smile.

"I like that idea," Cameron leaned over and said kissing his wife.

"Great! I'll make reservations at our favorite restaurant for Friday," Diamond beamed, extra giddy, nuzzling Cameron's neck.

"Sorry, babe, this Friday won't work. Let's do Saturday instead."

"I looked at your schedule. I thought you didn't

have any games this weekend?"

"We don't, but since we have a few days off, Andrew is having his bachelor party that night."

"Oh, that should be fun. You want me to tag along with you?" Diamond teased.

"Sorry, no wives allowed," Cameron grinned. "But no worries, I'm coming home to you." He pulled Diamond down on the bed.

"Don't you have practice?" Diamond asked as Cameron started pulling down her lace panties.

"I do, but I can be a little late." He gave a sly smile before his face disappeared between her legs.

"Ah... ah... ah," Diamond moaned, leaning her head back and closing her eyes. Cameron's tongue felt like a magic stick with each stroke on her clit.

Diamond arched her back as her body began to relax, welcoming the pleasure. Right when she was about to have an orgasm, Cameron stopped and slid inside her wet walls. The intensity of it all caused Diamond to clench her nails into his back while wrapping her legs around his lower torso. The deeper Cameron went the more forceful Diamond's grip became. She didn't believe she could love her husband any more than she already did, but his sex game always made Diamond feel like she was falling in love again for the very first time.

"They'll be ready for you in five minutes," the creative assistant told Blair as she was about to answer her phone.

"Okay, I'll be there in one second," Blair replied before focusing her attention on her call. "Hey, babe! How are you?"

"Going crazy missing you. I feel like we've been playing phone tag since you've been gone," Kirk complained.

"I know. The hours on set have been so crazy. But I've been missing you too. I can't wait to get home."

"When will that be?" Kirk wanted to know.

"Tomorrow is our last day shooting and flight leaves that following day. I can't wait to see you and Donovan. What have you been doing since I've been gone?"

"Besides missing you, just practice. Hanging out wit' Cameron a lil' bit, but..."

"Blair, you need to wrap that conversation up. We need you," Skee walked up and said, causing Kirk to stop mid-sentence.

"Who is that?" Kirk questioned, thinking the tone of the voice sounded familiar.

Blair put her finger up. "Give me one second. Here I come."

Skee paused and stared at Blair for a moment then walked off.

"Answer the question, Blair. Who was that?"

Blair hesitated for a few seconds. She decided it was best to come clean with Kirk now because he would find out anyway once the commercial was released. "Skee."

"What the fuck is Skee doing there!" Kirk barked. He was so loud Blair moved her head back so the ringing in her ear would stop. "Answer the fuckin' question!"

"Kirk, calm down."

"Don't tell me to calm the fuck down."

"Listen, I had no idea until I arrived on set that Skee was the headline artist for this commercial. What was I supposed to do?"

"Walk the fuck off the set. That's what you shoulda did. So, he been there wit' you since you got to LA?" he grilled.

"Like I said, he's the star of the commercial so yes, he's been here and it would've been completely unprofessional of me to walk off the set just because I have to do a commercial with my ex," she huffed.

"So, you care more about some bullshit commercial than yo' man?"

"Excuse me?! What does one have to do with the other?"

"You know how I feel about that motherfucker! You shouldn't even be in the same city wit' that nigga, let alone working wit' that foul fuck."

"Kirk, you need to calm down."

"Blair, we really need you on the set. Everyone is waiting for you," the creative assistant came and said, as if slightly irritated that Blair was holding things up.

"Kirk, I really have to go. We can talk about this when I get back to my hotel room."

"No, we gon' finish talkin' about this shit right now!" he demanded.

"Everyone on the set is waiting for me! I have to go. I'll call you back as soon as I can. Bye."

"Blair! Blair!" Kirk kept yelling out until he realized she had ended the call. "FUUUUUUUCK!!!!!" he roared about to throw his iPhone against the wall, but he caught himself and stopped. "I can't believe she's in fuckin' LA wit' Skee," Kirk seethed, pacing back and forth. "Yo, I need to catch a flight to LA right now!" he continued venting his thoughts out loud trying to decide what his next move should be. The only thing that brought his huffing and puffing to a halt was when he noticed Cameron was calling him.

"Yeah," Kirk growled in the phone.

"Kirk that you?" Cameron questioned thinking maybe he had called the wrong person.

"Yeah, it's me," he snarled, still breathing heavy.

"You a'right over there... what's wrong wit' you, man?"

"Can you believe Blair over there in LA doing that commercial wit' Skee fuckin' ass! I'm 'bout to get on the next flight outta here and bring her home."

"Kirk man, chill. I know how you feel about Skee, but she over there working. Let her do her job and then she's coming home to you." Cameron was trying to be the voice of reason.

"Fuck that shit! I didn't want her doing that commercial in the first place. Ain't like she need the money. She need to be home takin' care of our son. Instead she three thousand miles away wit' that scum."

"When is Blair coming home?"

"She's supposed to be back Saturday."

"Listen, go wit' me to Andrew's bachelor party tomorrow night."

"Damn, I forgot about that shit." Kirk shook his head.

"You can't miss that. The whole team showing up. We gotta show our support. "

"I guess." Kirk shrugged not caring the least. He was too preoccupied thinking about what Blair was doing.

"Stop stressing about Blair. We'll hit the party then you can come to that spot wit' me again so I can do a lil' gambling. Get yo' mind off all this Skee shit and have some fun. Got me?"

"Yeah, I got you. But when Blair get back home, I'm putting an end to all this Hollywood shit. She gon' be a wife and mother. That career bullshit is over," Kirk spat.

"Damn, I can't believe we gettin' a few stacks a piece just to go to a freakin' party!" Yaya giggled excitedly, flipping through the hundred dollar bills in her hands.

"We gotta fuck too," Taj said, admiring her own stacks.

"We do that anyway so what are you sayin'." Yaya side-eyed her as if Taj sounded slow and stupid.

"Don't get too excited, cause ya don't get the rest until after you perform," Lyric reminded the women.

"Girl, you don't have to worry about that. Performing is our favorite part," Monroe said laughing. "It used to be yours too, until you got wifed up," she added.

"I ain't that nigga's wife," Lyric said frowning.

"Then why ain't you workin' this party wit' us so you can get paid too?" Monroe questioned.

"Don't play wit' me. You already know if you makin' coins then so am I. My cut is coming in the form of a finder's fee for locking you bad bitches down."

"Oh, so you our pimp now?" Taj chuckled.

"I guess you can call me that. Or better yet, call me a madam." Lyric smiled. "Nah, this a one time thing unless Packer wants to utilize ya's services again. Ain't shit free." Lyric winked.

"Packer still ain't told us what we doing at this party. Do you have any idea?" Yaya wanted to know.

"Besides the fuckin' part... nah. You know I'ma keep it one hundred. All he told me was he wanted three bad chicks and the pay was excellent," Lyric told them.

"Honestly I don't care. He gave us spending money to buy new outfits for this shindig and we getting paid too. Shoooooot," Taj smacked. "As long as niggas ain't runnin' no trains on a bitch, I could give a fuck."

"Rigggggggght," Monroe and Yaya chimed in.

Lyric sat back on the bar stool and listened to her girl's chatting it up. A few months ago, she would've been leading the conversation, being extra hyped about what she would've called a cute come up. But now, Lyric was over the shit. Being with Packer had made her lazy to the hoe shit. Servicing one nigga and have him take care of all your needs was a lot more convenient than constantly being on the prowl for the next trick.

Lyric's relationship with Packer would be the perfect fit except there was one need Packer couldn't satisfy and that was Lyric's desire for the limelight. She craved that almost as much as money. That was the only reason she caught an attitude when Monroe said she had gotten wifed up. There was no doubt Lyric was looking to become wifey, just not to a drug kingpin like Packer, but for now he would have to do.

Chapter Ten

The Plot Thickens

"It's a wrap!" Those words were music to Blair's ears. She loved being in LA doing the Apple commercial, but she was anxious to get back home to her son and Kirk.

"You did great." The male voice caught Blair off guard, as she was taking off her damn near seven-inch heels that had her ready to chop her feet off.

"Thank you." She gave a half smile and turned away.

"I'm Gerad Lang," he called out, following behind Blair.

"Nice to meet you," she turned around and said. His name sounded very familiar, so Blair figured he was part of the crew that worked on set.

"I remember that Denzel Washington movie you were in a couple years ago. It was a small role, but you made a major impact. I was wondering whatever happened with your career. It was as if you disappeared, so it was a pleasant surprise to see you doing this commercial."

"I had a baby and wanted to be a full-time mom. Now I'm trying to get back into acting."

"I see. Well a national commercial like this is a great look for you. This is huge."

"Thank you. Are you part of the crew?" Blair asked.

"Oh, no. I'm an agent with Elite Talent Agency."

"That's why your name sounded so familiar. Wow, they're major."

"Yes, we're the top talent agency in Hollywood and I would love to have the opportunity to represent you."

"Excuse me?!" Blair gasped. Her mouth dropped, but she quickly picked it up. "I wasn't expecting you to say that."

"I don't see why not. I'm always on the search for the next big breakout star and you have a ton of potential. I believe with my help and your talent, I can take you far."

"Mr. Lang..."

"Call me Gerad," he jumped in and said.

"Gerad, I am so honored that an agent of your

caliber is even interested in representing me, but I already have representation."

"Oh really... which agency?"

"Glitz Inc."

"Yeah, I've heard of them. That's Kennedy's company." Gerad nodded his head.

"That's right." Blair smiled.

"Isn't that a PR firm... not a talent agency?"

"True, but she does some management also. I mean, she got me that Denzel movie and this commercial which you said yourself was huge."

"You're right, that's very impressive. I have some female clients I was angling to get on this commercial. It's one of the reasons I showed up. I wanted to see who the lucky girl was that managed to avert my plans."

"That would be me!" Blair playfully raised her hand. "And it's all thanks to Kennedy. So again, although I appreciate your interest, my loyalty is to her. But again, thank you so much."

"Loyalty is rare in this business. I hope Kennedy appreciates that quality in you. Things do change and if you're ever in the market for a new agent, please give me a call." Gerad handed his business card to Blair which she took with reluctance.

"So, you met Gerad." Skee came up and said while Gerad was walking off.

"You know him?" Blair questioned.

"Who doesn't know Gerad. He's one of the

biggest agents in the business. If Creative Artists wasn't treatin' me so good, I would definitely fuck wit' dude. So, what did he want wit' you?"

"He wanted to be my agent," Blair said coyly.

"Word! That's dope. You about to have Gerad Lang as your agent. You big time!" Skee beamed.

"No! I declined."

"Why the fuck would you do that?"

"Kennedy is managing my career. Even Gerad acknowledged she's doing a damn good job because she got me this commercial. So, I'm good."

"I know Kennedy is yo' homegirl and you wanna look out for her, but be careful wit' that."

"Be careful with what?"

"It's not always good to mix friendships with business. Shit can get messy quick. I'm not sayin' that's gonna happen with you and Kennedy, but keep your options open," Skee advised.

"I get what you saying, but Kennedy has my back."

"Cool, so umm you wanna go do dinner?" Skee asked changing the subject.

"I can't. "

"Why not? I know you hungry."

"I'll order some room service when I get back to my hotel."

"Why don't we have dinner at the restaurant at your hotel," Skee suggested.

"That won't work." Blair was looking in every

direction except directly in Skee's eyes.

"What's going on with you?" Skee lifted Blair's chin and turned her face so she was facing him.

Blair let out a deep sigh before answering. "That phone call I was on yesterday, that held up shooting, well it was Kirk. He heard your voice and wanted to know why you were with me."

"When you told him we were doing the commercial together he went ballistic," Skee huffed not needing Blair to tell him the rest.

"Exactly. We spoke last night and I told him it was strictly business between us. I'm supposed to call him when I get back to my room so we can finish hashing things out. We already ran late and I'm sure he's wondering why I haven't called him yet. If we go out to dinner, it will only make a bad situation worse and I don't want to lie to him."

"I find it amazing that you have this man's child, you live together, yet he still sees me as a threat. Why do you think that is?" Skee reached out, grasping Blair's wrist, anticipating her response.

"I'm not going there with you, Skee. I'm with Kirk. He's the father of my child and I'm determined to make it work." Blair freed her arm leaving Skee frustrated as she hurried off.

"I guess that means you won't be flying back with me tomorrow on my private jet," Skee scoffed.

"Yo' girls ready for tonight?" Packer asked while he sat on the couch watching the money machine count his paper.

"My girls stay ready although they are wondering what they supposed to do tonight. Hell, I'm curious too," Lyric admitted. "I guess I'll have to wait and get all the details after the party."

"Nah, you'll be right there to see for yourself."

"Huh? I didn't know I would be attending the party wit' you."

"You're not attending wit' me, you'll be escorting them. This work, not pleasure."

"Why I gotta go babysit them? This yo' project. Ain't you gon' be there?"

"Nope! I don't wanna put anyone on notice. I need that nigga to be relaxed. If I show up, he'll be outta his comfort zone."

"Who are you talkin' about and what that got to do wit' me going to the party?" Lyric folded her arms then rolled her eyes as she wondered what bullshit Packer was up to.

"You wanna make this money don't you?" Packer knew Lyric's weakness was them dead presidents, so he dangled that shit in her face.

"Of course, but you gon' have to add a few more

stacks to yo' bill if you want me to chaperone some grown ass women."

"I got you!" Packer tossed Lyric some money that was rolled up. She caught it with one hand like a pro baseball player. "Good catch," he said, nodding his head in approval.

"Now explain to me why I have to escort these chicks tonight." Lyric was irritated she had to attend a party that required her to watch over her friends, instead of participating in some fun.

"I was gonna wait until later, but I can tell you now. I need you to listen very carefully and follow my orders to a tee. If anything goes wrong, I'm placing the blame on you. So, don't fuck this up," Packer warned.

"Listen, I ain't one of yo' workers slingin' dope on the corner block. Tell me what I need to do, so I can collect these coins and be done wit it," Lyric's sassy ass spit.

Packer let out a slight chuckle. He wondered what he liked better about Lyric, her feisty attitude or the bomb head she gave him. "I'ma start calling you my lil' soldier girl."

"That's funny. Now, can you get to talking? If I'm going to this party I need to find something to wear."

"I got you. This is how everything is going down tonight," Packer leaned and said as Lyric listened intently. Her eyes widened in disbelief as she heard the convoluted plan Packer had come up with. She had been around him long enough to know that Packer hated to be embarrassed. But she never would've guessed he would take it this far because he felt clowned by Cameron. Lyric knew this wouldn't end well for anyone involved, but getting that money outweighed any of her hesitations.

Chapter Eleven

Why Didn't You Come Home...

"I feel like you just got here. I can't believe you're leaving already." Kennedy sighed before taking another bite of her veggie omelet.

"I know right! On the bright side, at least we get to have breakfast together before I leave to catch my flight."

"Yeah. This was a business trip, but it would've been nice if we could've hung out a little. Who knew commercials could be so time-consuming."

"I have a newfound respect for commercial

actors now," Blair said nodding. "I'll admit, it was fun."

"Did reuniting with Skee have anything to do with it?" Kennedy gave Blair an inquisitive stare.

"Maybe a little. I always have fun with Skee. He gets me, unlike..." Blair's voice trailed off.

"Unlike who... Kirk?"

"Basically. He called me while I was on set and heard Skee in the background."

"Boy, I know that didn't go well," Kennedy remarked, taking a sip of her mimosa.

"He was screaming at me on the phone like I'm his child. I thought we worked things out, but I called him last night when I got back to my hotel room and he didn't answer. I eventually fell asleep, but when I woke up this morning, I didn't have any missed calls from him so he never called me back. I sent him a text before I came down to meet you for breakfast and he hasn't responded."

"You know there's a three-hour difference. He's probably still sleep," Kennedy reasoned.

"True, but I think he's still just pissed about Skee."

"Does he think you all hooked up?"

"He didn't come right out and say that, but he for sure alluded to it. That's why I need to get back home and try to make things right."

"You don't sound too optimistic." Kennedy could see the stress written all over Blair's face.

"I love Kirk, but he wants a housewife and I want a career. Hopefully, we can find a happy medium."

"I hope so too because the work is about to start pouring in for you. If Kirk is having a hard time dealing with things now, it's only going to get worse."

"I'm determined to make things work with Kirk. I want to keep our family together," she said with sincerity. But how much was Blair willing to give up, to make that a reality?

When Diamond heard the front door open, she rushed from the kitchen to the foyer. "Cameron, where have you been? I was worried sick about you."

"Baby, I'm so sorry." He walked over and kissed Diamond on her forehead. "I promise you I wasn't planning on staying out all night."

"Then, why did you?"

"By the time Andrew's bachelor party ended, I was so drunk, there was no way I could get behind the wheel of a car. So, I crashed at the spot he had the party."

"Why didn't you at least call and let me know? It's the middle of the afternoon, Cameron!"

"I misplaced my phone then when I found it once I woke up, the battery died. Yo, I ain't neva been this fucked up. I can't remember shit. I need some water. I'm dehydrated like a motherfucka," Cameron mumbled heading to the kitchen with Diamond right behind him.

"You went to the party with Kirk, why couldn't he bring you home?" Diamond questioned.

"That nigga was fucked up too. Everybody was fucked up," Cameron said shaking his head.

"So you saying..."

"Hold up." Cameron put his hand up, cutting Diamond off. "Before you start interrogating me wit' a million questions, can I at least take a shower and take some aspirin for this fuckin' headache I got."

Diamond tightened the tie on her sheer pink silk kimono as she stared her husband down. He seemed off, but she couldn't put her finger on it. To her, Cameron appeared to be suffering from more than a standard hangover. Diamond was pissed that her husband didn't come home last night, but it was his teammate's bachelor party and under no circumstances would she want him to drive drunk. But the more she tried to rationalize his behavior the angrier she became. Diamond didn't want to come off as the nagging wife, so she let it go for now.

After Cameron went in the bedroom, Diamond placed a call to her bestie Blair.

"Hey girlie!" Blair answered.

"Hey! Where you at? I hear a lot of noise in the background."

"At the airport. My flight just landed and I'm finally back in New York."

"Oh, wow. How was your trip?"

"It went great."

"Good! You'll have to tell me all about it over dinner."

"That sounds nice. We haven't done one of those in a minute," Blair said looking around for her car service.

"Yeah. So, have you spoken to Kirk? Is he picking you up from the airport?" Diamond was fetching for information, but with Blair just getting back in town, she wasn't sure how helpful she would be.

"No. He's a little upset with me," Blair admitted.

"Why?"

"I'll give you the long story over dinner, but the short story is, he found out I was doing the commercial with Skee. I haven't spoken to him since Thursday night."

"Are you serious?"

"Very. I tried calling him a few times last night and got no answer. I sent him a couple of text messages this morning and got no response. I'm home now, so we'll work it out."

"I'm sure you will. But umm, when you get

home and settled, call me so we can set up that dinner date."

"Will do! Talk to you later."

"That was a bust," Diamond moaned, putting her phone down. "More than likely Cameron was telling the truth about being with Kirk. If Blair couldn't reach him last night or this morning, he was probably passed out drunk too," Diamond said out loud, trying to figure the shit out. She wanted to let it go and justify it as a boys' night out, but the knot in the pit of her stomach wouldn't allow it.

"I get money, money I got!" Taj belted out the car window as she sped down the street.

"Bitch, that shit was lit as fuck last night. Shiiiit, I would've worked that party for free," Yaya said laughing.

"But why party for free when you can get paid!" Taj was still screaming out the window, enjoying having a pocket full of money. Packer just hit the ladies off with the remaining balance due, now that their services were complete. So of course, they were ready to celebrate by spending and posting their newfound cash on social media.

"Hold up, turn the radio down! Let me get on Snapchat right quick," Monroe yelled from the backseat.

"Why didn't I think of that!" Yaya shook her head taking out her iPhone. While the ladies bragged on social media, Taj was gunning it on the Brooklyn-Queens Expressway, plotting on how her clique would get their next come up, since she knew this money was already spent.

Chapter Twelve

Welcome Home

Patience was one of many character traits Darcy Woods was severely lacking. She was growing increasingly frustrated that her scheme against Kennedy was turning out to be a major fail. She decided it was time to step her manipulation game up and put the ball back in her court. Darcy was waiting for the right moment to execute her latest shenanigans to bring Kennedy down and that opportunity was quickly approaching.

"I'm home!" Blair announced when she walked

through the door. She was expecting Donovan to come running out giving her a great big hug and for Kirk to be right behind him. Instead, the place was eerily quiet. Blair left her luggage by the door and ventured off to see where everyone was. First, she went to Donovan's bedroom. Everything was in order as if it had just been cleaned. She then went to her bedroom and found Kirk spread out on the bed knocked out. This wasn't the homecoming she anticipated.

Blair figured Donovan was with Jillian and they were out enjoying the beautiful day, while Kirk was still asleep in the middle of the afternoon. Instead of waking him, Blair decided to shower off the almost six-hour flight she just got off of. She didn't know whether to be disappointed or relieved that she got a moment to get fresh and clean in peace, before spending time with her son and Kirk. But she missed them both so much, especially Donovan.

Right when Blair was taking off her clothes to get in the shower, she heard a familiar sound coming from the sink counter. "Kirk must've left his cell in here before passing out," she commented out loud walking over to his cell, deciding to be nosey.

Last night was lit. We must do it again... Taj. The text message read.

"Who is Taj and what the hell did they do last night?" Blair mumbled out loud turning on the water. She was tempted to go back in the bedroom and toss Kirk's phone, knocking him over the head, but at the moment the hot running water was more appealing. "I'll deal with Kirk later," she decided.

"Your girls really came through last night," Packer commented to Lyric as they were getting dressed to head out.

"I knew you would be pleased. Let me know if you ever need them again, just as long as I get my fee," Lyric said smiling, putting on her sequin stripe bomber jacket over her striped wide-leg jumpsuit.

"I got what I needed. I should be good." Packer nodded. "It's good to know you game though," he said as he winked.

"So, where we going tonight?" Lyric asked, ready to switch topics since Packer wasn't entertaining putting any new money in her pockets.

"To visit a friend of mine."

"Oh." Lyric tried to hide her lack of enthusiasm. On the low she rolled her eyes, wishing she had saved her badass jumpsuit for a worthier occasion. She followed Packer out the door, hoping this would be a very short evening.

When they arrived at the location on the Upper East Side, Lyric immediately wondered what friend did Packer have that lived over here. She opted not to ask, but instead wait and see. As they entered the massive top floor oasis, Lyric was mesmerized by the three-level penthouse.

"Who the fuck lives here," she blurted. Before Packer could speak up, the question answered itself.

"What up, my nigga!" Skee cracked, hugging Packer. "It's good to see you."

"Good to see you, too. I ain't been over here since you first got the place. You got this place laid the fuck out." Packer nodded his head in approval.

"I can't really take credit. I hired this interior designer who hooked me up," Skee said.

"Well, she did a damn good job."

"She sure did," Lyric agreed, speaking in a tone so low she was surprised Packer heard her.

"Yo, Skee, this my girlfriend."

"Nice to meet you," Skee reached out his hand and said.

"Nice to meet you, too."

Lyric was doing a great job at keeping her composure, but she hated letting go of Skee's hand. It felt almost silky smooth like he had never done any hard work a day in his life.

"Come in here sit down. You the first to arrive. A few more people should be here shortly," Skee said, as Packer and Lyric took a seat on the couch.

"Good! That means we can chop it up before the rest of them clowns get here," Packer joked. "But seriously, what you been up to besides killin' these music charts."

"Same shit. I just got back from LA yesterday. I filmed a commercial for Apple. It was pretty cool. How 'bout you? You been staying out of trouble?"

"Man, you know trouble always find me." Packer laughed.

"I ain't surprised. You still be going to that gambling spot we used to hit up?"

"Motherfucka, you know it! I've been having a lil' trouble wit' this one nigga, but I got something fo' his ass," Packer boasted.

"I'm sure you do."

"Nah, I'm serious. I'ma teach this nigga a serious lesson. You'll neva guess who it is either."

Normally Skee would brush off what Packer was saying as he was known to talk shit, but he had piqued his interest.

Lyric watched from the couch as Packer and Skee walked off towards the wraparound terrace with the NYC skyline view. *Damn, why the hell I couldn't have landed a bona fide superstar like Skee Patron,* Lyric thought, shaking her head. *I mean fuck, this nigga out here living the life. I didn't even know Packer knew him. He would always drop little hints here and there that he had some big dogs on speed dial, but never did I think Skee was one of them. That was the thing about them celebrity drug dealers like Packer, they be running in the same circles with 'real' celebrities, but they can't put you in the spotlight like them,* Lyric said to herself with frustration. *I need this life, but I need to figure out how to make it happen,* she thought as she looked on intently at Packer and Skee.

"So, man, listen," Packer smirked pulling out his phone. "This NBA nigga kept testing me at them card games. I believe that motherfucka be cheating."

"You always say that shit every time you lose," Skee said, laughing. "Even as kids, when somebody in the neighborhood would beat you at any sport, you swear down they cheating." Skee continued laughing.

"They was cheating, you just didn't believe me! Just like this motherfucka cheatin' too," Packer insisted. "But after this shit hit. He ain't gon' have time to hit the gambling spot no more. Watch this!"

Packer shoved his phone in Skee's face, letting the sex video do the talking for him.

"Where did you get this?" Skee questioned, shocked by what he was watching.

"My girl filmed it for me." Packer turned and kissed at Lyric who was oblivious to what he was doing.

"What you plan on doing wit' this? Blackmailing dude?" Skee asked as he continued watching the video. Then his mouth dropped when he noticed another familiar face in the video being serviced.

"Nope. I'ma leak this shit online a few hours before their first playoff game next week. That shit gon' be epic. Maybe Cameron having all his business out here in these streets will humble that nigga. I even got his teammate Kirk in the video too," Packer bragged. "Them niggas definitely gonna lose the game that night," he chuckled.

"Delete this shit. Now!" Skee demanded.

"Huh?" Packer frowned.

"You can't leak this video and whatever copies you got, get rid of them. I mean that shit, Packer."

Packer had known Skee long enough to know when he wasn't bullshitting and this was one of those times. "Why do you care?"

"Because I do. I shouldn't even have to explain myself to you. When mottherfuckas turned they back on you, when they thought you was gon' do a bid, who stepped up and saved yo' ass?" Skee pressed.

"I didn't mean it like that, man. I know I can neva repay you for all you've done for me. No doubt I owe you and if you want me to delete this video then that's what I'll do. All I want to know is why."

"Because Cameron's wife is best friends with a woman who is very special to me and Kirk is her man."

"Damn!" Packer's eyes widened in disbelief. "That shit wild," he kept saying, as he shook his head. "If she's special to you, then you need to let her know how her man gettin' down. I'll delete every copy of the video and I promise not to leak it, but before I do, I'm sending a copy to you. I'll let you decide what to do with it," Packer stated.

Chapter Thirteen

Lying In Wait

"I'm so glad you were able to meet me for lunch. I feel like we haven't hung out in forever," Diamond said taking a bite of her salmon.

"I know. Since getting back from LA, trying to work things out with Kirk has been taking up so much of my time. Spending time with you was much needed... trust me." Blair sighed.

"How's that going?" Diamond wanted to know.

"I never realized a relationship was so much work. It's like having another job except it's not so easy to quit especially when there is a child involved," Blair admitted.

"I know what you mean. I find myself brushing

things off with Cameron just to keep the peace."

"Me too. When I got back from LA, I saw this cryptic text someone sent Kirk. I was tempted to ask him about it, but I just let it go."

"What did the text say?"

"Last night was lit. Let's do it again, or something like that," Blair shrugged. It was from some chick named Taj."

"She must've been talking about that bachelor party him and Cameron went to," Diamond determined.

"What bachelor party?"

"One of their teammates. It was on a Friday and you came back Saturday."

"That makes sense. When I got home, it was the middle of the afternoon and Kirk was in the bed knocked out."

"Cameron didn't even come home that night. He showed up still out of it the next afternoon. He said he was too drunk."

"What did you do? I would've been livid."

"I was!" Diamond barked. "I might be calm right now, but I was pissed. But I decided to let it go."

"Why?"

"Because I've learned you have to pick and choose your battles if you want to make a marriage work!" Diamond exclaimed, tossing her hands up. "Maybe Cameron did have too much fun at the party, but I'm sure he didn't take it too far."

"What do you call too far?"

"Sticking his dick in another woman's pussy." Diamond rolled her eyes. "That would be a game changer."

"It sure is. I still haven't gotten over Kirk cheating on me."

"Kirk cheated on you... when... and why am I just hearing about this? Was it recently?" Diamond leaned in close, pushing her plate to the side.

"It was about a year ago. He was on the road. He claimed it was a one-time thing, he slipped up and it would never happen again," Blair smacked her lips as if she didn't even believe the words coming out her mouth. "I wanted to tell you, but I was so angry. I knew talking about it would only make it worse."

"Blair, I'm so sorry. I hate that you dealt with it on your own. That had to be hard. I'm glad you decided to work things out with Kirk though."

"I don't know. When the trust is broken, it's hard to get things back to where it used to be and needs to be. That's why I didn't accept Kirk's proposal."

"Girl, Kirk asked you to marry him! Damn, you been holding out on me!" Diamond hollered before lowering her voice when she realized people in the restaurant were staring. "I can't believe you turned Kirk down."

"Diamond, I don't want to marry a man I don't trust. Wouldn't you leave Cameron if he cheated on you?"

There was an uncomfortable silence. Then Diamond reached for her glass of wine and took three long sips. "It isn't that simple, Blair," she finally said. "We have two small kids. With Rico being dead, Destiny thinks of Cameron as her father. Cheating isn't worth breaking up my family for," Diamond rationalized. "I think you should marry Kirk. He loves you, Blair, and you have a sweet, beautiful son together."

"I don't know if I'm cut out to be an NBA wife… a wife period. I want to be a star."

"You say that now. But remember. You can be a star today and a nobody tomorrow. There are no guarantees in Hollywood," Diamond scoffed.

"True, but there are no guarantees a marriage will last either," Blair shot back before downing her own glass of wine.

The two best friends spent the remainder of their lunch with fluff talk. In their heads, both were replaying the words exchanged and neither wanted to admit the unknown had them shook to some degree.

"Girl, it was wonderful spending time with you. I missed my best friend," Diamond said giving Blair a hug as they stood outside the restaurant.

"Me too. We can't go this long without some quality girl time again. Now all we gotta do is get Kennedy's ass up here, so it can really be like old times." Blair smiled.

"Yes! We must make that happen soon. Do you want me to give you a ride back home?" Diamond offered.

"No, thanks. I'm actually headed to the gym. It's right around the corner. That's why I'm carrying this enormous purse," Blair commented, lifting it up. "I have my workout clothes and shoes in here."

"Oh, and I thought you were just being fashionable," Diamond joked. "Okay, well off to the gym you and let's talk later. Bye, chica!" Diamond and Blair exchanged air kisses and headed in opposite directions. From a short distance, Blair had no clue that Darcy had been lying in wait, anticipating the perfect opportunity to make her move.

For the last week or so, Darcy had been trying to pinpoint Blair's daily routine. She called it watching her target, but it was more like obsessive stalking. She had concluded that Blair went to the same gym to work out, if not every day than close to it at the exact same time. That's why she was thrown off for a second when she spotted her prey dressed in an embroidered denim jacket, nude slinky bodysuit, relaxed low-rise jeans and a pair of strap wedges instead of her normal workout gear. Darcy soon realized she was meeting someone for lunch.

"Yes, say goodbye to your silly bestie," Darcy huffed as she watched the two women hugging. "I don't know who is dumber you or Diamond," she cracked waiting to see what Blair's next move would be. To her delight, she realized that Blair was a little off schedule time-wise, but would be sticking to her normal routine of hitting the gym.

The day before, Darcy had already secured herself a free gym pass by pretending she was interested in joining. Although she had no intentions of breaking a sweat unless it was servicing Michael sexually.

After Blair entered the gym, she waited a few minutes before grabbing her bootleg workout gear from her car and heading inside. She went straight to the women's locker room and pretended to be stunned when she ran into Blair.

"Oh, gosh, I guess they're letting anyone join so-called exclusive gyms these days," Darcy smacked, brushing past Blair.

"No need to diss yourself, Darcy. Low self-esteem isn't a good look on anybody. Enjoy your workout." Blair batted her eyes and gave a quick wave.

"Wait!" Darcy called out before Blair exited.

"What is it?" Blair stopped and asked. "I really don't have time to engage in a battle of words with you."

"You're right. I'm sorry. I was being immature and petty," Darcy said in a sincere voice.

"Did my ears hear you correctly... did Darcy Woods just apologize to me? I must be hearing things."

"No, Blair you heard right. My comment was completely unnecessary. I guess after all this time, I'm still salty that you were the girlfriend and I was the other woman when it came to my relationship with Michael. That's hard for me to admit."

"Wow! The surprises from you keep coming. Where is all this change of heart coming from?"

"Honestly, I've been taking anger management classes for the last couple of months," Darcy lied and said. "Part of getting better is acknowledging when you're wrong and try to make things right. I know we'll never be friends, but I at least want us to be respectful to one another. Especially since now that I'm getting back into PR we'll probably be running in the same circles on occasion."

"Yeah, you're right, we'll never be friends, but I think respectful is doable." Blair gave Darcy a half-smile.

"Great! Oh, and congrats on the Apple commercial. That's huge!"

"Thanks! I'm surprised you heard about that already. We just finished shooting it."

"I still have a lot of friends in the business. That was a big win for you. So many agents were trying to get their clients that gig. Good thing your ex is still carrying a torch for you."

"What does that mean?" Blair gave Darcy a baffled look.

"I'm talking about Skee personally choosing

you to star in the commercial opposite him. Once that happened, it shut down any other actress's chance of landing the part. There's no need to be embarrassed. Deals based off relationships are done every day. You're a beautiful girl. Skee did nothing wrong wanting to use his ex-girlfriend instead of some random chick."

"You must be mistaken. Kennedy landed me that part, not Skee."

"Oh, no!" Darcy put on her best stunned and mortified face. "I thought you knew it was Skee. Honestly, I figured you must've asked him to do you the favor after Kennedy let that other actress have your movie role. I must admit you really are a loyal friend to keep Kennedy as your publicist and manager after she did that to you."

"Darcy, what the hell are you talking about?" Blair screamed.

"Clearly, I've said too much. I need to get dressed so I can go work out. Excuse me," Darcy said in a timid tone.

"You're not going anywhere!" Blair shouted, grabbing Darcy's bony wrist. "You need to explain yourself."

"Blair, I was under the impression that everything I said you already knew. Clearly, that's not the case, so I don't feel comfortable talking about it anymore."

"Please tell me everything you know about that

movie role and Skee getting me the commercial. I need the truth," Blair pleaded.

"Well, if you insist...."

Blair's pleas were music to Darcy's ears. She had played her hand like a pro and Blair fell perfectly into her trap. The two women, who less than fifteen minutes ago wouldn't have thought twice about lighting the match to set the other on fire, were now enthralled in a deep conversation. They sat down on one of the benches in the lady's locker room as Darcy revealed all. Except, of course, the role she and Michael played in the scheme. On the inside, Darcy was smiling with glee as she set Blair's ears on fire with the details of Kennedy's betrayal.

Chapter Fourteen

Seeking The Truth

"You've been in a good mood for weeks now. I love seeing this side of you. It reminds me why I've been in love with you for all these years even when we were apart." Sebastian reached over, taking Kennedy's hand an d placing a soft kiss on it before then kissing her lips.

"That's so sweet. I had been in a major funk, but business is finally starting to pick back up and I have a feeling it will be booming soon," Kennedy beamed. "With me getting the word out that Blair is about to star in the new Apple commercial with Skee, the offers are really starting to pour in."

"I knew you could do it. You're a go-getter.

With your determination, you'll always come out the winner."

"You have no idea how much your support means to me. I never want to disappoint you." Kennedy put her head down.

"You could never disappoint me," Sebastian assured her, lifting Kennedy's head back up. "Having you back in my life has been the best thing that's ever happened to me. Dylan even loves you."

"I love him, too. You really do have an amazing son."

"I'm glad you think so because I was hoping you'll stick around for the long haul." Sebastian then got down on bended knee before pulling out the ring he had in his pocket. "Kennedy, would you do me the honor of becoming my wife?"

"Yes! Of course!" Kennedy cried. "Ohmigosh! The ring is so beautiful." She placed her hand over her mouth in astonishment as Sebastian slipped the one-of-a-kind, handmade, platinum and 18k yellow gold, cushion stone diamond ring on her finger.

"I have the man of my dreams. My business is flourishing again; my life can't get any better than it is now. I thank God every day that you're back in my life."

"I love you so much," Sebastian held her tightly in his arms and said.

"I love you, too." The tears continued to flow as Kennedy held on to her future husband, knowing he was the only man she wanted to spend the rest of her life with.

"You never told me why you decided not to release that sex tape," Lyric mentioned casually while they sat on the couch halfway watching some bullshit reality show. She knew if she seemed too interested, Packer would become suspicious and not tell her shit. So, Lyric waited an entire two weeks before asking him again, hoping to catch him off guard so he would spill all the details. Luckily, it somewhat worked. Packer didn't give her all the answers, but he told Lyric just enough for her to connect the dots.

"My man Skee asked me to dead it. Some chick he checking for is best friends with that nigga Cameron's wife."

"Lucky for Cameron, but what a waste of time for you."

"Skee's request put a dent in my plans but I'ma fix that motherfucka." Packer sounded confident, but he wasn't giving Lyric any clues on how he intended to pull it off.

"I'm sure you will."

"But hey, at least I put some chump change in you and yo' girl's pockets," he chuckled before tossing some popcorn in his mouth. "You did delete that video, didn't you? I gave Skee my word that there were no more copies."

"Yes, that video has been deleted. It's not even in the clouds," Lyric said without hesitation. "You really care about what he thinks... huh?"

"You damn right! Skee a good dude. Wit' all that fame and fortune he got, he still that same nigga that grew up wit' me in the hood."

"So, the two of you grew up together."

"Yep. I was a couple years older than him, so he was like my lil' homie, but we were close. Then those teenage years kicked in and I went one way selling dope and he started gettin' into that music shit. Didn't nobody even take his ass seriously." Packer let out a loud laugh. "We used to clown that nigga when he said he was writin' rhymes and he would be a rapper. We watched that nigga blow up and the joke was on us."

"That's crazy. It goes to show you should never underestimate someone."

"True dat." Packer nodded in agreement. "When you put yo' mind to something, you can make shit happen."

Lyric sat on the couch with her arms folded, soaking in everything Packer said. He had no idea that what he thought of as a funny little story he decided to share got the wheels spinning in Lyric's head. The same way the hood underestimated Skee, she felt that Packer and everyone else miscalculated what she was capable of accomplishing too. Lyric was more determined than ever to prove them all wrong.

"Blair, come in. I was surprised when you called saying you needed to see me. Especially after the way we left things in LA." Skee closed the door, but Blair remained silent. "Would you like to sit down?" he questioned, trying to break this weird vibe Blair was giving off.

"No, I don't need to sit down."

"She speaks!" Skee announced then started clapping his hands.

"Funny," Blair smirked. "I'll admit, I'm acting a little strange. I've been debating with myself for the last few days and concluded, if I wanted the truth then I needed to ask you directly."

"Okaaay... so ask."

"Skee, don't lie to me. I want you to be completely honest. Do you promise to do that?"

"Whatever you're about to ask me seems to be very important to you."

"It is. That's why if you care about me, you won't lie even if you believe I'll be upset."

"You know I care about you, so yes, I promise to tell you the truth."

"Did you get me the Apple commercial?" The grimaced expression on Skee's face said it all, but that wasn't enough for Blair. She wanted to hear him say it.

"Who told you that?"

"It doesn't matter. Answer the question... you promised, remember."

"Yes, I got you the commercial. But Blair..."

"Don't but me," she barked cutting Skee off. "I so badly wanted it to be a lie, but in my gut, I knew it wasn't." Blair shook her head with discontent. "Why? We hadn't seen each other or had any contact for over a year. Why did you feel the need to bring me back into your life now?"

"I saw you at the GQ party."

"You were there... I didn't see you."

"I know. I had them seat me in a corner booth. I wanted to keep a low profile. But when you walked in," Skee sighed, "all these feelings came flooding back. I thought I was over you, but instead I wanted you back."

"So, you put the call in for me to star in the commercial with you."

"I figured if we spent some time together, the same way I realized I wanted you back, you would want me back too," Skee confessed.

"I can't believe this. The only reason I got that job was because of you. Not because of my talent or hard work, but because of my ex-boyfriend," Blair scoffed.

"Blair, you are talented. I knew you would be perfect for the part and I was right. Everyone on set loved you."

"As if they would tell you otherwise, especially since you're the one that made it happen. Were you ever going to tell me the truth?"

"No. I didn't want you to feel like you owed me anything. If you still had feelings for me, I wanted them to come from the heart, not out of obligation."

"Skee, I'm not going to stand here and pretend like I don't care for you. I've accepted the fact that I probably always will. But I told you, I'm committed to Kirk and making our family work. Now so more than ever. I'm starting to think that Diamond is right and I should listen to what she said."

"What did Diamond say?"

"That there are no guarantees in Hollywood. You can be on top one day and a nobody the next."

"Blair, that's with anything in life. There's always risk, but at least you're following your passion. Don't give up on that."

"Please! If it wasn't for you, I would be on the front of some hair relaxer box right now." Blair turned her head in frustration. "Maybe it would be for the best if I married Kirk and became an NBA wife. At least I would know it was real instead of a make believe Hollywood career."

"No! You can't do that... you can't marry Kirk."

"I know how we feel about each other, but Kirk is the father of my son and I do love him."

"But you love me too."

"I do, but Kirk can give me the stability that I need so I can focus my attention on being a good mother to Donovan."

"Blair, you can be a good mom to your son and still pursue your career as an actress. I want to help you with that. I believe in your talent. I always have. Plus, don't be so sure that Kirk can provide you with that so-called stability you claim to want."

"What is that supposed to mean?"

"Since this is supposed to be a conversation based on truth, then let's put it all out there."

"I thought that was what we were doing."

"Are you sure you're ready for the truth... all of it? No matter how ugly it might be. Can you handle that?"

"Yes, I'm positive."

"Then watch this." Skee grabbed his phone off the table and pulled up the video Packer sent him. When Packer initially tried to give him the video, Skee declined, but now he was thankful he took his friend's advice.

"What am I about to watch?" Blair wanted to know.

"You'll see in a second. Then, you tell me, is this the man you think will bring you stability and deserves to call you his wife."

Blair felt like she was about to hyperventilate. She backed up, falling on the couch as she covered her face in despair. "Where did you get this?"

"From a friend of mine. This all went down at a bachelor party for one of their teammates. I know those types of gatherings can get a bit out of hand, but this is a full-fledged sex video."

"Diamond is gonna be devastated. Cameron is her world. That marriage has already endured so many obstacles."

"Luckily I convinced my friend not to release it. I have the only copy and now that you've seen it, I'ma delete it."

"Are you sure he deleted it and there are no more copies?"

"Positive. He would neva cross me like that."

"Why did he make this anyway? Was he planning on extorting them?" Blair questioned.

"Nah, he just wanted to release the tape right before the first playoff game. He wanted to embarrass Cameron. They both heavy into this gambling shit and Cameron got my dude feeling some type of way. This was supposed to be some payback shit."

"I would hate to get on your friend's bad side. He goes hard."

"Yeah he does, but I know how close you and Diamond are. I couldn't let him do that to you or her," Skee said.

"Thank you so much. Not only for looking out for Diamond, but for also revealing the ugly truth to me. Seeing is truly believing."

"I know showing you this video might seem cruel. But I couldn't let you give up your dreams and build this life with Kirk without having all the facts. Now you know the truth. It's up to you to decide what you want to do with it," Skee stated.

Blair wanted to turn it off and erase all the images from her mind, but her eyes kept finding their way back to the video. Her feelings were crushed and her heart was broken. She knew Kirk wasn't perfect and their relationship had flaws, but visually seeing your man fuck another female was another type of pain. It was something no woman should ever have to see. Now that Blair had, her relationship with Kirk would never be the same again.

Chapter Fifteen

Letting Go

"Baby, after the playoffs are over, I want us to go on an extended vacation. Anywhere you want. You decide," Cameron said zipping up the last of his luggage to hit the road with his teammates.

"Are you serious?" Diamond was surprised and excited by what Cameron said.

"Very. I know we haven't been spending quality time together and I wanna change that."

"That would mean the world to me. Lately, you've been so distant. I miss my husband."

"I know babe. I'm sorry. I've been under a lot of pressure with the playoffs. My mind ain't been right," he conceded.

"I understand." Diamond walked over to Cameron and gently stroked the side of his face. "You focus on the game and I'll plan our vacay."

"You know you mean the world to me, right?" Cameron stared deeply into Diamond's eyes as if searching for approval.

"Of course, and you mean the world to me too. Our family is everything to me. As long as we have each other then we can get through anything."

"You my ride or die, foreal." Cameron smiled.

"Now and forever." Diamond rose up on her tippy toes to give her husband a kiss. "Now you go get on that plane and kick some major ass in Indiana. I'll be right here cheering for you."

Diamond walked Cameron to the door, kissing each other one last time before exchanging I love yous and saying goodbye. For the first time in weeks, Diamond felt like she had her husband back.

"I finally have my Cameron back." Diamond leaned up against the door beaming. "Now where should we go on our vacation?" she questioned out loud getting on the computer to do a Google search. "A romantic remote island sounds nice." But before she could even type it, she noticed Blair was calling her. "Hey, girl!"

"Hey. Are you going to be busy later? I wanted to stop by if that was okay."

"Of course, you can stop by. I would love to see

you. I'll order us some food and we can drink our favorite wine."

"You don't have to do all that," Blair said. "No need to go through all that trouble."

"Don't be silly! What trouble?" Diamond laughed. "Delicious food and expensive wine is no trouble at all. So, what time are you coming over?"

"Around 5, but I'll text you when I'm on the way."

"Cool! I'll see you then."

Blair let out a heavy sigh when she hung up with Diamond. Ever since Skee showed her the video, she had been debating whether to tell Diamond about Cameron. Initially, she decided to keep it to herself because she didn't want to ruin their marriage, but Diamond was her best friend. She had the right to know the truth.

"Babe, I'm 'bout to head out. Come give me a kiss goodbye," Kirk said standing at the door with his luggage.

Out of everything, putting on a charade with Kirk was the most difficult. Blair was relieved that would be coming to an end today.

"Blair!" Kirk hollered again, wondering where the hell she was.

"Sorry about that. I was finishing up my conversation with Diamond."

"Cool, well come give me a kiss so I can go get

on this plane."

"That won't be happening," Blair stated.

"Huh?!" Kirk gave her a perplexed stare.

"I mean, you will be getting on the plane, but I won't be kissing you ever again."

"What the fuck is you talkin' 'bout?" Kirk appeared agitated, dropping his Le Mans large holdall bag to the floor.

"I'm talking about that chick you fucked at that bachelor party a few weeks ago."

"What chick?"

"I'm assuming it was Taj. Since she sent you a text the very next day."

"Man, I don't know what you talkin' 'bout, Blair. I don't know no Taj and I didn't fuck nobody at Andrew's bachelor party." That was Kirk's story and for a very short moment, he was sticking to it. Until Blair dropped the receipts.

"I saw the video, Kirk. You and Cameron were doing plenty of fuckin' that night, so save your lies."

Kirk's face frowned up like he had been sucker punched in the gut. His head fell, looking down at the floor, closing his eyes.

"Video... there's a video?"

"Yes, there is."

"Blair, I can explain."

"Save it."

"The day before I found out you were in LA

wit' Skee. I didn't know what the fuck was going on between the two of you. All sorts of shit was runnin' through my head."

"We were working while you was fuckin'! But you wanted to think the worse. Find an excuse to do the same reckless shit you've done in the past. I forgave you once, but not this time," Blair spit. "And by the way, if it wasn't for Skee that video would be everywhere by now."

"I don't understand."

"Of course, you don't." Blair rolled her eyes in disgust. "But it doesn't matter. The damage is done."

"I fucked up, but I promise to make this right, babe. Whatever I have to do."

"There is nothing you can do. When you get back from your road trip, Donovan and I will be gone."

"What?! You can't leave... the two of you don't have no place to go."

"That's where you're wrong. I've been getting things in order for the last week. I found a temporary apartment for us to stay at until I can find something more permanent. You're free to spend as much time as you like with our son, but you can co-ordinate that with Jillian. There is no need for you to contact me."

"Blair, you can't do this." Kirk grabbed Blair's arm, but she yanked it away.

"Don't touch me! Don't ever touch me again!"

"Baby, I love you. I fucked up... I made a mistake, but don't break up our family because I did some dumb shit."

"We are not a family. Donovan is your son. I'm simply the mother of your child. So, you better go ahead and leave before you miss the plane."

"Baby, please don't do this!" Kirk pleaded in vain as Blair walked away to gather her belongings.

Chapter Sixteen

Begging For Mercy

"Kennedy! Please tell me you're calling because you just arrived in NYC and you want me to come pick you up." Diamond said cheerfully.

"I wish, but soon, I promise. Right now, I'm in work mode and trying to track down my client Blair. I haven't been able to reach her for the last week. I've left her a ton of messages."

"That's not like Blair. But since she got back from LA, she has been trying to work on her relationship with Kirk... maybe," Diamond's voice trailed off.

"Gosh." Kennedy let out a deep sigh. "We're making so much progress. Please don't let Kirk ruin it."

"I'm not saying that, but like I told Blair, Kirk is a sure thing, Hollywood not so much."

Kennedy stopped twirling around in her chair and immediately took Diamond off speakerphone. "I know you're not filling Blair's head with that garbage!"

"I'm telling her the truth. She has all these big ideas about being a movie star and we both know the odds of that happening are slim to none."

"Says who? Blair has the looks the talent and for the last couple of months she's had the drive. But between you and Kirk that drive might be dissipating as we speak." Kennedy shook her head becoming stressed at the very idea.

"Kennedy, calm down. I'm not disagreeing with you, but Blair has a son to think about. All I'm doing is giving her realistic options."

"You're trying to highlight the option you chose, Diamond. Maybe Blair isn't interested in being another NBA wife."

"Kennedy, I have to go now. Blair is coming over later today and I'll tell her to call you. Bye!"

Kennedy let out a loud scream when Diamond hung up on her. With all the work she had lined up for Blair, the last thing she needed was any interference. Things were going too good to allow them to go bad now.

Cameron was getting comfortable in the swivel chair, relaxing his legs on the footrest and about to use his iPhone app to control the television screen, until Kirk disrupted that.

"Man, you awfully calm for a nigga who just got caught out there," Kirk remarked.

"What the fuck are you talkin' 'bout?" Cameron shrugged.

"The video of us having sex wit' those chicks. If Blair saw it, I know Diamond has."

Cameron damn near spit out his vitamin water. "Video! There's a fuckin' video?" Cameron's heart began racing.

"Yes."

"Diamond didn't mention anything before I left home and she hasn't called me. She must not know yet."

"Then either she bullshittin' you or she ain't seen it. But get ready 'cause Blair will be spillin' it soon. I guarantee you that," Kirk nodded.

"Maybe it's not too late. Call her!"

"Call who?"

"Call Blair right now before the plane takes off."

"She ain't gonna answer. She so pissed wit' me."

"Then I'll call her from my phone. What's her number?" Cameron was dialing as Kirk was spitting the numbers. He was praying Blair would answer.

"Hello."

"Blair, it's me... Cameron."

"Cameron, what do you want?"

"I'm not sure what you think you saw, but..."

"But nothing. I know what I saw," Blair huffed. "I have to go..."

"Don't hang up!" he called out in desperation.

"What is it?"

Cameron could hear the irritation in Blair's voice and knew he had to be straight up if there was any chance of getting through to her. "That night was really crazy. I was drunk. So, drunk that I barely remember what happened. I'm not excusing what I did, but I don't wanna hurt Diamond."

"You should've thought about that before sexing some other chicks," Blair shot back.

"Have you already told her?" Cameron wanted to know.

"Not yet, but I'm telling her today."

"Blair, I'm begging you not to do that. I know Diamond is your best friend, but she's my wife. We have two beautiful kids. Don't destroy that because I fucked up. Please, Blair."

"I'll think about what you said, Cameron, but I can't make any promises. I have to go."

Cameron rested his hand over his face. "How the fuck did I get myself in this situation," he mumbled.

"I take it your conversation didn't go well with Blair," Kirk figured.

"I don't think it did. Blair said she would think about not telling Diamond, but it sounded like she was just trying to get me off the phone."

"Maybe you'll be better off calling Diamond and telling her first," Kirk suggested.

"Honestly, I thought about that, but I can't bring myself to hear the pain in Diamond's voice if I told her the truth. Please God, let Blair have mercy on me," Cameron prayed.

"So what's next on our list? Are we hittin' up the official after party for Kendrick Lamar's concert or what?" Monroe asked while touching up the polish on her fingernail.

"I'm down. Just let me know when so I can get my outfit on deck." Yaya was geeked.

"Girl, we already know yo' ass down," Taj smacked, getting a can of coke from the refrigerator. "I ain't tryna go to some after party to listen to some music. I can do that shit right here from home. If we can't make no money then nah, I ain't interested."

"Well, I got the official hookup with a booth in the VIP section."

"Word! Who hooked you up wit' that?" Yaya wanted to know.

"None of yo' damn business," Monroe scoffed. "The point is, we'll be sittin' lovely wit' all the rich niggas. So to answer your question, Taj, yes there is money to be made."

"Good, 'cause I'm sick of living in this small ass apartment. I'm due for an upgrade," Taj frowned, flopping down on the sofa.

"At least you got yo' own crib. I'm still in the same cramped bedroom I grew up in, at mother's house," Yaya complained munching on chips. "I need to find me a man to lockdown like Lyric did."

"I know what you mean. All these random sponsors is wearing my pussy out. I'm on the search for a permanent sponsor my damn self. I even hit up that nigga Kirk McKnight."

"That basketball player from the bachelor party?" Monroe wanted to confirm.

"Yes. The way I fucked and sucked that nigga, I was positive he would be begging for a follow-up."

"And you ain't heard nothing from him... damn!" Yaya shook her head.

"No, I did hear something from him, but not what I was expecting."

What did he say?" Monroe put her polish down, more interested in what Taj had to say.

"He sent me a text cursing me the fuck out about that video of us fucking."

"How did he see that? Lyric said Packer deaded everything and deleted the video," Monroe said.

"I guess it wasn't deleted after all. After he hit me up I called Lyric and asked her what was good. She said she would speak to Packer and get back to me, but I ain't heard shit."

"Wow, that's fucked up," Yaya said, chiming in.

"I ain't worried about that shit. I'm more pissed that nigga was pressed about a video of us fucking instead of us linking back up," Taj sighed taking the last few sips of her soda.

"Fuck that nigga, Kirk!" Monroe yapped. "We in New York. He ain't the only motherfucka wit' long paper. If you really lookin' for a rich nigga to take care of you on a long-term basis, you'll find one. Lyric got her come up and you will too. So we going to this party or what, ladies?"

"Motherfuckin' right!" Taj and Yaya shouted simultaneously.

Chapter Seventeen

Buried Secrets

"Blair, are you listening?!" Diamond questioned loudly. Putting her hand on Blair's leg.

"Of course I'm listening," she said giggling, trying to play it off.

"Then which one, Fiji or French Polynesia?"

"Which one for what?" Blair had this puzzled, bewildered expression.

"Duh! For my getaway vacation with Cameron. I knew you weren't listening." Diamond pouted. "What's going on with you, Blair? You've been acting strange since you got here. Obviously, something's on your mind. What is it?"

From the moment Blair walked through the

front door and sat down, she started and then stopped herself from telling Diamond the truth about Cameron. The fistfight that was taking place between her mind and heart had turned savage. Blair's brain was begging her to tell Diamond the ugly details about the video she saw, but her heart pleaded that she keep it a secret. Listening to Diamond go on about how excited she was to go away with her husband also didn't help.

"Diamond, I'm fine," she lied. "I have a lot going on so my mind is a little frazzled. Sorry."

"Does this have anything to do with work and Kennedy? She called me earlier looking for you."

"Really... what did she say?"

"That she had been trying to get in touch with you for about a week and you haven't returned any of her calls. She said she had a lot of work lined up for you. She was a bit concerned that you were giving up on your career as a Hollywood star. Is that true? I mean, have you decided to take my advice and marry Kirk so you can become a part of the Basketball Wives Club." Diamond smiled.

"Honestly, that's what I came over to talk to you about."

"OMG!!! I knew it! You took my advice and accepted Kirk's proposal. Show me the ring! No need to hide it. I know the secret now!" Diamond clapped her hands with anticipation of the big reveal.

"Diamond, I'm not marrying Kirk. As a matter of fact, Donovan and I are moving out. I've already found us a temporary spot until I find something long-term."

Diamond's mouth dropped and for a few seconds she was speechless. "I don't understand. When we had lunch, you said since being back from LA your focus was making your relationship work with Kirk and making your family stronger. What happened?"

"That was true until I found out he cheated on me again."

"What! Kirk cheated again... are you sure?"

"Positive. I saw the video." Blair sighed still hurt and unable to get those images out of her head.

"You actually saw a video of Kirk having sex with another woman?" Diamond's eyes widened in disbelief.

"Yes!" *I also saw your husband doing the same fuckin' thing!* Blair said to herself, but was unable to say those words out loud.

"I'm so, so sorry, Blair. That has to be beyond painful." Diamond leaned over on the sofa and hugged Blair. "I'm here for you. We'll get through this," she said, rubbing Blair's back trying to console her.

"Thank you so much, Diamond, but there's more. I..." Before Blair could reveal that Cameron also had a starring role in the video, Diamond interrupted.

"It's one thing to think or even know that yo' man cheated, but to see that shit in color. I would lose my fuckin' mind if Cameron did some shit like that to me. I popped out a baby for this nigga. Hell, you know what I mean. You popped out a baby for Kirk's ass too," Diamond huffed, shaking her head. "I need a drink just thinking about the fuckery of it all," she hissed standing up. "I'll pour you one too."

Right when Blair thought her mind had won the fight, her heart came out swinging. She started thinking about all Diamond had been through: from her trifling ass baby daddy Rico, who treated her like shit, to the wedding that almost didn't happen. Diamond also going to jail, being kidnapped, and then shot by Lela, who left her paralyzed. After surviving one brush with death, nearly being killed by that psychopath Sharon who had a paternity test switched so it showed Cameron as the father of her child. Only God knows how they survived one tragedy after the next, but they did. Even Diamond's fear that she would never be able to give the man she loved more than anything in this world a child, but against all odds that happened too. Blair wasn't sure if Diamond could survive more heartbreak and she definitely didn't want to be the cause.

"Here," Diamond said handing Blair a glass of wine before sitting back down. "While I was pouring our drinks, I realized how insensitive I had been. I was going on about my vacation with Cameron and how happy I was now that my marriage seemed to be back on track, all the while you're going through all this drama with Kirk."

"Diamond, you didn't know, so you weren't being insensitive. Yes, I am hurt, but I'll get through this. It's better I know the truth now instead of walking down the aisle and realizing later I married the wrong man," Blair reasoned.

"So, this woman you saw in the video with Kirk, was it a one-time thing or is ongoing?" Diamond questioned.

"I think it's a one-time thing, but why does that matter?"

"Listen, I think what Kirk did is foul and he needs to be held accountable for the bullshit he's putting you through, but..."

"But what?" Blair interjected.

"But I know he loves you and Donovan. Men make mistakes, especially professional athletes. I personally think they all need chaperones. I mean temptation is real and it's constantly being thrown in their faces. If I didn't have two small children to take care of, I would definitely be on the road with Cameron."

"Are you worried he might cheat on you?" Blair asked.

"Of course! I'm not stupid, but I also know that Cameron loves me and our family. He wouldn't want to destroy that. Plus, with all we've been through, he knows I couldn't survive that sort of betrayal. A heart can only take so much before you snap." Diamond looked away for a second, then gulped down the rest of her wine.

"I really need to go," Blair said feeling guilty and uncomfortable.

"So soon?"

"Yeah, I need to pick up Donovan. I still haven't told him that we'll be living in a new place without his dad."

"That's going to be tough. Are you sure this is what you want, Blair? It's not too late to change your mind and try to work things out with Kirk."

"It is too late. I'm done with Kirk and the sooner we move out the better. I'll call you. Take care of yourself, Diamond," Blair said giving her best friend a hug goodbye.

"You, too. Call me if you need me."

After Diamond closed the door, Blair stood outside with her hand pressed against it for a moment, tempted to go back inside. *Let it go. You're doing the right thing. Some secrets are best kept buried,* Blair thought as she walked away.

"I was surprised when you said you were in LA," Barry said, regretting he agreed to meet Darcy for lunch before their meal was even served.

"I'm expecting to have lots to do in LA very soon," Darcy beamed. "I thought it was the perfect time to get back on the Hollywood scene. Make my presence known."

"Don't you think that's a bit premature? From what I'm hearing, Blair has quickly become a hot commodity. So, I seriously doubt Kennedy will be having problems making her payments anytime soon," Barry affirmed.

"Is that the sound of enthusiasm I hear in your voice, Barry?" Darcy questioned with a bit of disdain as she placed her mint colored AQ trench on the chair next to her. She then flicked a light piece of debris off her matching Roland Murray dress while sizing Barry up.

"I could care less one way or the other. I was only sharing information that I perceived as beneficial to you."

"I think they fitted your custom Italian suit a little too tight because you're not even trying to be convincing with your lie. You do care, but unfortunately you care about the wrong person. I'm disappointed in you, Barry. I thought we were friends."

Barry's eyes darted around in a condescending way. "Our relationship isn't based on friendship, it was us fulfilling a mutual need."

"Your need for your client to get a role that had slipped through her fingers until Blair was taken out the equation. Now you need to deliver on my need."

"I've been doing my part, Darcy. I don't have the power to sabotage Blair's career."

"But you do have the power to get me invites to the events where all the industry elite will be."

"As I stated, don't you think it's a bit premature to start reconnecting with the bigwigs when you don't have a business or any clients," Barry smirked.

"I'm more than confident that will all be changing soon. Now do your part and I'll handle the rest," Darcy sniped.

"I'll line some things up for you. How long will you be in town?"

"For the foreseeable future."

Barry wanted to wipe the smug look plastered across Darcy's face. He hated himself for even agreeing to be a part of her scam, but Darcy was smart. She knew Barry's thirst to remain relevant in such a cutthroat industry would sway him to jump at the opportunity to give one of his client's a plum role in a major movie and also put some much-needed cash in his pocket. Now Barry was stuck doing business with a woman he couldn't stand.

Chapter Eighteen

No More Lies

Blair had spent the last few days getting her and Donovan settled into their new place. It was a bit cramped, but the location was great and she kept telling herself it was only temporary. While organizing her closet, Blair was cleaning out one of her purses and came across a forgotten about business card.

"Gerad Lang of Elite Talent Agency," Blair said reading the business card. "I think it's time I stop putting this off." Blair grabbed her phone before going in her bedroom and sitting down.

"Blair! Where have you been?" were the first words out of Kennedy's mouth when she answered her phone. "I've been trying to get in touch with you for two weeks."

"I've had a lot going on."

"We have a lot of work to do. This isn't the time for you to go missing. Unless Diamond was right and you've decided to focus on Kirk instead of your career," Kennedy pried.

"This has nothing to do with Diamond and no I'm not focusing my attention on Kirk. So, you said we have work to do. Does that mean you have a job lined up for me?"

"Several. A couple are auditions for some major movie roles and some are well-paid modeling jobs, another is a lead in an Indie movie. There is also a commercial on the table for a major brand," Kennedy stated.

"Another commercial. Speaking of commercials... how did you get me the one for Apple?" Blair asked, seeing if Kennedy would be truthful.

"Just doing my job. Making phone calls, sending out your press packages, getting the word out about you. It paid off and Apple took notice and now so are a lot of other people."

"Really. It's amazing how it all came together so seamlessly. I wonder why it couldn't have gone the same way for that movie role. Why do you think, Kennedy?"

"Excuse me," Kennedy said after coughing. "I had something caught in my throat.

Yeah, you got something caught in your throat alright, a fuckin' lie, Blair thought to herself as she got up from her bed.

"Blair, I'm so sorry about that movie role. I know how much you wanted it to happen."

"You have nothing to be sorry about. It's not your fault I didn't get the part... right?" At this point, Blair was sick of listening to Kennedy's lies. She was praying she would tell the truth, but Blair realized that wasn't going to happen.

"I know it's not my fault, but I still feel bad. You're my client. When things don't work out for you, I always feel guilty," Kennedy explained.

"Are you sure that guilt isn't because you sold me out?" Blair shot back.

"Blair, what are you talking about?"

"Let's start with how Skee was the one who got me the Apple commercial, not you. I could've let that go though, Kennedy. What I can't let go is the deal you made with Barry Alston which cost me a movie role that should've been mine."

"Blair, I don't know what..."

"Stop the lies, Kennedy! Are you seriously about to tell me it isn't true?!" Blair shouted cutting Kennedy off.

"I can explain."

"Now you want to explain after being busted. This phone call was all about me giving you an opportunity to explain, but instead of doing so you just tried to feed me one lie after another."

"I honestly didn't know Skee got you the part. I'll admit, once I realized he was the artist in the commercial, I did put two and two together."

"So why didn't you admit that instead of fabricating some bullshit story?"

"Because I knew I had fucked up with the movie and I felt this was my chance to make things right," Kennedy said.

"You didn't make anything right, you only made things worse. I can't even trust you anymore. Not as my publicist, manager, or even my friend."

"Blair, I had no choice about the movie role. It was either that or I was going to lose my company. A company that I've busted my ass for."

"So you sacrificed me to save yourself."

"It wasn't like that. I didn't have a choice."

"More lies. You always have a choice, Kennedy. You chose yourself and now I'm doing the same. I'm no longer your client and you'll never make another dime off me again."

"Blair, wait!" Kennedy yelled out, but Blair had already hung up.

Wasting no time, Blair's next call was to Gerad Lang. While Kennedy's next call was to Diamond.

"Kennedy, I've been meaning to call you. I hated how things ended the last time we talked," Diamond said as she drove to Queens, on her way to see her mother.

"Don't worry about it. I was calling because I wanted to speak with you about Blair."

"You still haven't spoken to Blair? I gave her your message a few days ago. She did just move so she's pretty hectic right now."

"Blair and Kirk moved again? They just got that penthouse a couple years ago. Why are they moving so soon?" Kennedy wondered.

"Don't say anything to Blair until she mentions it to you which I'm sure she will next time you all talk."

"Mention what?"

"Blair left Kirk. She found out he cheated on her," Diamond sighed.

"Again! Wow, first Michael, then Skee, now Kirk. Blair has the worst luck with men. So unfortunate," Kennedy exhaled feeling bad for Blair.

"I think Blair should try and work things out with Kirk. He loves her and they share a child together."

"Who cares! If Kirk doesn't love Blair enough to respect her, then she doesn't need him!" Kennedy exclaimed.

"But they belong—"

"Diamond, let's table the stand by your man conversation for another time," Kennedy said before Diamond could go on a long testimony to validate her point. "I called you to discuss something much more important."

"Fine! What is it?" Diamond snapped, annoyed that Kennedy interrupted her.

"Blair is really upset with me right now and she has every right to be. She fired me and I really need your help to mediate the situation."

"What exactly did you do?" Diamond questioned.

"I took credit for getting Blair the Apple commercial when it was actually Skee. But initially, I had no idea he was the one that got her the part, but—"

"You eventually figured it out. Instead of being honest with Blair you embellished," Diamond stated. Using the opportunity to return the favor by now cutting Kennedy off mid-sentence.

"I wouldn't use the term embellish, more like—"

"Lied." Diamond remarked.

"I wasn't completely honest and can you please stop cutting me off and there's more," Kennedy hated to admit, but she knew Blair would spill it all soon so she figured it was best to come clean with Diamond.

"I'm listening," Diamond said as she parked in front of her mom's house, waiting to go inside until after Kennedy gave her all the details.

"A few months ago, I was really struggling financially with my business. I thought I was going to have to shut down. I couldn't get a loan from my bank and it had gotten so bad that I needed money

ASAP. I reached out to a friend mine, Barry who is also in the business. He agreed to help me out, but I had to give him something in return."

"Which was?" Diamond was ready for Kennedy to just spill the tea instead of taking her on the scenic route.

"Remember the movie role that Blair thought she had on lock?"

"Of course, I remember. Blair was devastated about that. I had never seen her so upset."

"Part of the deal I made was to tell the movie producer that Blair could no longer do the role because of another commitment. That way Barry's client who was up against Blair for the part that would get it."

"What! How could you do that to Blair?!" Diamond yelled into the phone.

"I know it was foul, but everything I worked so hard for was slipping through my fingers. When you decided you could no longer be a part of the business because you wanted to focus on your family, everything fell on me."

"Oh, so now it's my fault that you fucked over Blair!"

"I'm not saying that. I'm trying to explain how I ended up in this predicament. My overhead was high. After Blair had her baby she wasn't taking on any new gigs and the few clients I did have weren't bringing in enough money to cover all my expenses.

Initially, when we partnered up, you were the money person and I had the connects. It takes time for a business to get off the ground. With you no longer being in the mix, everything fell on me." Kennedy said, defending her actions.

"Why didn't you come to me for the money then?"

"Diamond, I did reach out to you. Remember that week I was blowing up your phone and you never returned my phone call?"

Diamond thought back and she did recall that period. She was dealing with her own issues and speaking to Kennedy wasn't a priority. "I remember, but that still doesn't excuse what you did to Blair. I understand why she fired you. I would've too."

"I called you, Diamond, because I thought you would be a little more understanding since you had to make deals with a drug kingpin to save yourself. Or have you forgotten that life now that you've become accustomed to living in luxury off your husband's millions?"

"Is that jealousy I hear in your voice, Kennedy?"

"No! What you hear is a woman who has had to work her ass off for everything. I've never asked for handouts or thought pushing out a baby for a rich man would mean I'd never have to work a real job a day in my life. Your only concern is holding on to Cameron. You could care less about my problems. So don't sit on this phone judging me for making a mistake like you haven't fucked up before!" Kennedy barked.

"I'm not about to sit on this phone and listen to you ridicule me for putting my family first. No one told you to take yo' ass to LA, sniffing behind Sebastian. You shoulda asked yo' fuckin' man for the money instead of screwing over Blair. Now you have to face the consequences. Just like Blair is done wit' you, so am I!"

Kennedy didn't know if she wanted to scream or cry. She had gotten dismissed and hung up on by both of her friends within the same hour. She couldn't wrap her mind around how everything went so bad so fast. Just a week ago Kennedy was ecstatic that her life seemed perfect. She was engaged to the man she loved. Her business was finally on track and within a matter of minutes, it seemed to be going downhill. For some strange reason, Kennedy thought it was only about to get worse.

Chapter Nineteen

The Countdown Begins

"I wish you would've called before you came over because Jillian is at the park with Donovan. They won't be back for another twenty minutes. You can come back then to pick him up," Blair told Kirk when he showed up unexpectedly.

"Or I could wait here until they can get back," Kirk suggested. "It is only twenty minutes."

"Fine. You can have a seat," Blair reluctantly agreed.

"How have you been? With you having Jillian bring Donovan to my place, it feels like I haven't seen you in forever."

"Yeah, it's been almost two months now since

we've seen each other. Putting space between us was necessary. I needed some time to clear my mind. But I've been good."

"Cameron wanted me to tell you, thank you for not telling Diamond about the video. He genuinely appreciates you doing that for him."

"I didn't do it for Cameron. I did it for Diamond and part of me still feels guilty for not telling her the truth."

"Then why didn't you?" Kirk was curious to know.

"Because the day I went to tell her, she looked incredibly happy," Blair said, glancing out the large window that had a view of the busy New York City street. "I didn't want to be responsible for taking the smile off her face which meant me keeping Cameron's secret."

"For what it's worth, I think you made the right decision."

Blair didn't bother responding so Kirk switched the subject. "The apartment is nice," he commented, glancing around since this was the first time he was seeing her new place.

"Yeah, I like it, but I spoke to my realtor yesterday and the place I really want will be available in a couple of months. So, there's no need for us to get too comfortable."

"True. But there's also the other option. You and Donovan could come back home where you belong."

"That's no longer my home. When I said we were done, I meant it."

"How can you throw it all away like that? I fucked up, but you know we belong together."

"The only thing I know is you've cheated on me at least twice in the last year. I'm over it. I've invested enough time into this relationship. I'm ready to move on."

Before Kirk could respond, they heard the front door opening. Jillian and Donovan were back. "Daddy! You're here!" Donovan ran up to his father giving him a hug."

"That's right, lil' man." Kirk lifted his son up in the air. "You ready to spend the weekend wit' me?"

"Yes!" Donovan beamed with excitement.

"Great!"

"I'll go get his bag," Jillian said, heading to Donovan's bedroom.

"Mommy, you should come spend the weekend with Daddy and me too," Donovan said smiling. "Right, Daddy?"

"I think that's a great idea." Kirk nodded.

"Not this time, baby. Mommy has lots of work to do. You go have a great time with your dad and I'll see you Sunday night."

Blair walked over and gave Donovan a hug and kiss. Seeing Kirk holding their son did tug at her heart. Although she had her reservations, Blair made up her mind they would be a family and now she would be denying Donovan what he wanted most. It would be easy for her to give in and go back to Kirk, but she knew they'd be living in a home full of unhappiness. That wouldn't be a healthy environment for anyone, especially their son. Blair had to let go and no one was going to change her mind.

Kennedy had been avoiding Barry's calls for the last week as she scrambled to get her money together for the payment she owed. Since she hadn't been late and consistently paid on time, Kennedy was hoping Barry could extend her due date. Knowing it made no sense to prolong the inevitable any longer, she placed the call.

"I was beginning to think you were avoiding me," Barry said when he answered his phone. "I'm glad you decided to return my phone call, Kennedy."

"My apologies. I've had a lot going on, but that's no excuse for me not calling you back sooner," she replied earnestly.

"It's not a problem. You've always been on time so you're a week late, I can cut you a break," Barry chuckled.

"Can that break last an additional week?" Kennedy nervously flipped her pen on a notepad waiting for Barry's response.

"Kennedy, if I could extend it for a week I would, but the most I can do is three days max."

"Come on, Barry. I haven't missed a payment in four months. That should be worth something."

"It is. That's why I'm giving you an additional three days when you're already a week late."

"Please, Barry!" Kennedy pleaded.

"I can't. It's not my money!" he blurted out in frustration.

"What do you mean it's not your money?" This was the first Kennedy was hearing of this and it threw her off.

"I borrowed the money from someone else."

"Why didn't you tell me that? I thought I was borrowing the money from you."

"What difference does it make? You would have to pay regardless. You think because we're friends, you wouldn't have to pay me back?" Barry asked.

"I didn't mean it like that. I thought you would be more flexible, more understanding of my situation."

"Kennedy, when you told me you were having financial problems, I wanted to help."

"You also wanted your client to get that movie role which she did thanks to me. Somehow Blair found out about the deal I made with you and fired me. I've been hustling my ass off to make sure I didn't miss a payment even though it's going on two months since Blair has been my client."

"I'm sorry to hear that, Kennedy. I really am. But like I explained, it's out of my hands. He's already agitated that you're late on your current payment."

"Maybe if I explain to him what's going on, he'll be more understanding. Why don't you let me talk to him?" Kennedy suggested.

"No!" Barry shouted. He quickly lowered his voice, upset that he had lost his cool. "I'm sorry, Kennedy. There's nothing I can do. If I don't have your payment by the end of the business day on Friday, then you'll be in default of the loan."

Kennedy didn't say another word. She ended the call and put her head down on her desk. The walls were closing in and Kennedy felt boxed in a corner. She only had one option and she hated it more than anything. *How do I even explain to Sebastian how bad things have gotten for me, without him seeing me as a failure. But at this point I don't have a choice. If he can't help me, then I'm done,* Kennedy thought to herself as she continued resting her head on her desk, wishing this was nothing but a bad nightmare that she would wake up from at any minute.

"Baby, I'm heading over to Equinox for a workout. Call me if you need me!" Cameron yelled out before leaving out.

"Okay! Don't forget about our dinner reservations tonight!" Diamond ran out their bedroom and yelled to Cameron.

"You know I ain't gonna forget having dinner with my beautiful wife. Since you out here now, come over and give me a kiss goodbye," Cameron said smiling.

Diamond hurried over to the front door where her husband was standing and he leaned down placing a long, wet kiss on her soft lips.

"Damn, you look so sexy in those workout shorts and shirt. Plus, you're an amazing kisser. I have to be the luckiest person in the world," Diamond bragged.

"The second luckiest since I'm the first," Cameron countered. "Because without a doubt, I have the most remarkable wife ever. Now let me get outta here because if I look at you any longer in that pink negligée, it's coming off." Cameron gave Diamond a devilish smile, kissing her one more time before making his exit.

Diamond laughed all the way back to their bedroom thinking about what Cameron said. Ever since the playoffs ended he had been attentive and loving. It was as if he had become a new and improved husband. In a week they would be off on their romantic vacation and Diamond was not only looking forward to them relaxing on their private beach, but also making another baby in the process.

Chapter Twenty

Dreadful Day

On the rare occasions Diamond had the mornings to herself, she would spend them at Starbucks having chai teas and reading gossip blogs. This particular morning, she told Blair to meet her so they could play catch up before she left on her vacation with Cameron.

"Girl, I'm so glad you were able to meet me on such short notice," Diamond said once Blair arrived.

"Do you really think I was going to pass up an opportunity to chat it up with my best friend and get a caffeine fix at the same damn time!" Blair laughed.

"As you can see I already have your caramel

Frappuccino waiting for you." Diamond slid the drink over to Blair.

"Thank you, my love. So, what's going on with you this morning?"

"I'ma do a little shopping today to get ready for me and Cameron's vacation next week. I'm so excited, I can hardly contain myself," Diamond beamed.

"I know you are and I'm sure Cameron is too. Is he going shopping with you?"

"No. He's at the gym, making sure he keeps that body on point. Gosh that man is so fine. I still can't believe he's all mine." Diamond blushed. "Let me stop talking about my husband before I start getting all hot and bothered."

"Girl, you a mess." Blair shook her head laughing.

"I know," Diamond grinned. "So how is everything going with you and your new agent?"

"Good. I really like Gerad. I'm reading over this movie script right now that I'm auditioning for next week."

"Niiiiice!"

"Yeah, ever since that Apple commercial dropped the offers have really been pouring in."

"I knew they would. I mean you looked amazing in that commercial. I'm sure Kennedy is somewhere sick right now that she screwed you over. I can't get over that stunt she pulled," Diamond said with disgust.

"Neither can I. I really thought I was more than just a client to her. I thought we were close friends. But she showed her true colors. "

"From the sadness in your eyes, I can see you're still hurt."

"I am. I lost a dear friend, at least I thought she was."

"I lost a friend too, but good riddance to her," Diamond sniped. "You should've heard the way she was speaking. Demeaning my marriage and basically blaming me for her fucked up predicament."

"Hold on a second, this is Gerad calling me," Blair told Diamond before answering her phone. "Hey, Gerad... Gerad?" Blair called out a few more times before realizing the call failed.

"What's wrong?" Diamond questioned.

"The call dropped. The reception must not be good in here. I'ma go outside and call him back."

"Take your time! Gives me an opportunity to troll some of the gossip blogs and find out what's going on in these streets," Diamond said laughing.

"Okay, but this shouldn't take long. I'll be back in a minute," Blair said laughing along with Diamond.

"Let my nosey ass see what the hell is poppin' off," Diamond commented out loud as she used the Starbucks Wi-Fi to connect to the Internet. The second she clicked onto one of her favorite websites, regret set in. With Breaking News boldly displayed at the top, Diamond felt the life being sucked out of her. The coffee shop seemed to be spinning so Diamond held on tightly to her chair. She began to cough up her chai tea.

"Omigosh! Diamond, are you okay?! Here, drink some water," Blair said handing her a bottle. Diamond's breathing had become rapid and her face was beet red. "Drink it!" Blair yelled becoming petrified.

Diamond gulped down the entire bottle within seconds. She then got her breathing under control and the natural color of her face began to set back in. "I'm okay," she stated coolly.

"What happened? I step out for a couple minutes and I come back, you look like you were about to pass out." Blair was shaken to the core, but was trying to keep her composure.

"I'm fine," Diamond said matter-of-factly as if a light switch went off and she was back to normal. "I need to make a quick stop and I want you to ride with me."

"Sure." Blair agreed to go with Diamond, but she was puzzled. "Are you going to tell me what's going on with you?" she questioned as Diamond turned right on Lexington Avenue. But she got no response. Her best friend seemed to be in a daze but yet focused, if that made any sense. "Diamond, I really wish you would talk to me. This all seems weird."

Diamond remained on mute, so Blair just sat back and went with the flow, hoping her friend would snap out of whatever stupor she was in. The ten-minute ride was eerily silent until Diamond turned on East 92nd Street.

"You should get out the car," Diamond told Blair.

"Huh?" Blair raised an eyebrow and gave a "what tha fuck" face.

"Trust me, get out the car, Blair... now!"

"Fine!" Blair screamed back taking off her seatbelt. "Why the hell did you have me ride over here with you, if you were gonna kick me out the car?" Blair demanded to know as she closed the passenger door.

"So, you can pay my bail, in case I get arrested. If I don't get arrested, I'll be right back to pick you up." With that Diamond sped off while Blair yelled for her to stop. But there was no stopping her. Diamond was on a mission with her eyes focused on her target. That target was a custom chrome Lamborghini Cameron got for himself as a birthday present and Diamond was going to great pleasure in demolishing it. He had a prime parking spot near the Equinox gym so it was easy for her to locate his vehicle. She slammed down on the gas of her silver Mercedes AMG G63 SUV and rammed into the passenger door making a dent. But after slamming it repeatedly, Diamond put the car out of commission permanently and it was ready for a funeral.

By this time, a small crowd had gathered around with many of them filming the chaotic scene on their phones. They were all wondering who was the deranged woman behind the wheel. Blair on the other hand knew exactly who the woman was, but had no idea what unhinged lunatic had taken possession of her best friend. She wanted to reach in the car and drag Diamond out, but eventually it all came to a halt when her SVU shut down. She slammed it one too many times making her truck immobile.

"Fuck this Benz," Diamond shrugged before grabbing her purse and getting out. She stopped to get another look at the damage she caused and the widest grin appeared on her face. As Diamond stood relishing at the obliteration of Cameron's once prized Lamborghini, she heard Blair screaming her name. When Diamond turned to make eye contact with her, she was greeted by New York's Finest.

"Turn around and put your hands behind your back!" the police officer barked as his spit sprayed her face.

By the time Blair managed to get through the crowd, Diamond had already been handcuffed and placed in the back of the police cruiser. The crazy part was she appeared to be completely unbothered by it all as the cruiser drove away.

Kennedy was driving home, replaying what she planned to say to Sebastian. She wanted to choose her words carefully and prepare to have answers to any questions he might throw her way. Kennedy had no doubt Sebastian would give her the money. She was worried he'd grill her about why she let it get this far and hadn't come to him in the first place. They were engaged now and things were going so well, Kennedy didn't want an unnecessary rift coming between them.

"What the hell is going on?" Kennedy questioned out loud, banging her hand down on the steering wheel. Right when she got off the highway, the street was backed up. For about fifteen minutes the traffic was at a complete standstill. When it finally started moving it was at a very slow pace.

"Keep moving!" A patrol officer who was directing traffic yelled to the car that was in front of Kennedy. She turned to see what had caught the driver's attention.

"Oh wow! Somebody was in a bad accident." Kennedy shook her head, noticing a tractor trailer flipped on its side. Then she saw another car and began to wonder if it was a multi-car crash. "I hope everyone is okay," she mumbled turning her attention back on road. Kennedy then slammed down on her brakes, almost causing another accident when her eyes locked on a familiar vehicle that had also been involved in the accident.

Kennedy recklessly swerved out of traffic and pulled over to the side of the road, ignoring the horns blowing and the patrol officer yelling for her to get back in the car. She jumped out of her car, running towards the white BMW. Kennedy didn't want to believe the mangled sports car belonged to Sebastian, but in her gut she knew because of the rims. Her heart began to sink as she got closer to the scene of the accident where there were fire trucks and ambulances.

"That's my fiancé!" Kennedy cried realizing Sebastian was still trapped in his car and had to be extricated. Her knees became weak and the hot sun made her believe she was ready to faint. Unable to get any closer to the car, she watched from a distance as Sebastian's bloody body was removed from the vehicle and placed in the ambulance. Kennedy didn't know if her fiancé was dead or alive.

Chapter Twenty-One

The Spotlight

"Skee, what are you doing here?" Blair asked, sitting back down on the couch after letting him in.

"I'm sure you're upset after what happened to Diamond. I wanted to make sure you're okay," Skee explained.

"How did you find out Diamond was arrested? It only happened a few hours ago. Bail hasn't even been set yet."

"Diamond was arrested... for what?"

"If it's not about Diamond's arrest, then what are you talking about?" Blair was confused.

"You haven't been online today or watched the news?"

"No, Skee, I haven't. I was with Diamond then she got arrested and I spent the last few hours at the police precinct. I got home less than an hour ago, so logging on to the internet and turning on the television wasn't at the top of my to do list," she cracked.

"First, tell me why Diamond was arrested."

Blair let out a heavy sigh before answering. "I might as well tell you since you and everyone else will be hearing about it soon. Diamond took her SUV and used it to annihilate Cameron's Lamborghini in broad freakin' daylight. Can you believe that shit?!" Blair exclaimed, taking her fingers and rubbing them on her forehead as if trying to massage a migraine away.

"Yeah, I can believe it. If you saw a video of your husband fuckin' another woman, you would wanna wreck his shit too," Skee scoffed.

"What! I thought you said that video was deleted and there were no more copies! How could you let that happen?!" Blair roared.

"Yo, calm down. It wasn't the video Packer gave me. Cameron was on there with a different chick," Skee revealed.

Blair was completely stunned. "You're telling me there's a different video of Cameron having sex?"

"Yes, and it's all over the internet, social media, and even the news outlets are reporting on it."

"Omigosh," Blair exhaled speaking in a low monotone voice. "It all makes sense," she said laying down on the couch. "Poor Diamond. Her heart must be breaking right now." Blair's heart was breaking too as a single teardrop streamed down her cheek.

Lyric was sprawled out on the king-sized bed on the top floor penthouse suite at the Beverly Wilshire Four Seasons Hotel in Beverly Hills. She was on her second glass of champagne, enjoying the life as the newly minted internet sensation. All thanks to her starring role in the sex video with Cameron. Lyric was so caught up with living in luxury that she almost didn't hear the door.

"Just a minute!" she called out, taking her time strolling to the door like she was an A-list Hollywood movie star. "Darcy, just the person I wanted to see."

"You wouldn't know it by how long it took you to open the door," Darcy mocked, coming inside. "Do you have company?"

"No, why do you ask?"

"The scantily clad attire you're wearing."

"Oh, this." Lyric smiled, admiring the lingerie she purchased at a boutique in the hotel. "I like feeling sexy and wearing this does the trick."

"Whatever works," Darcy hissed. "But I'm here to discuss business, come sit down."

"I'm all about discussing business, especially if it means more money for my bank account."

"Money hungry clients are always the best kind. That means you're willing to do just about anything to be relevant," Darcy remarked.

"That would be me," Lyric boasted. Most would've taken Darcy's comment as a jab, but not Lyric. There was no shame in her game.

"Anywho, since the video leaked there has been a huge interest in finding out everything about you."

"I know! I mean my Instagram followers has skyrocketed. It's crazy."

"I'm sure it has and as I get your name out there more, it will continue to go up. There are several people that would like to interview you, but I'm not sure if you're ready for that," Darcy stated with hesitance.

"Why? I would love to do some interviews. We already did that photoshoot, so we have plenty of images to go along with it. Why not utilize them."

"That would work if we can control the questions and answers, but a live interview isn't a good idea. They will want details about how everything transpired on the night that video was made and from what you told me, that would open you up to some serious legal issues, which we don't want. Cameron's high priced attorneys are already trying to get the video taken down from some of the more popular websites by threatening to file a lawsuit."

"That's great! It means more publicity for me," Lyric beamed.

"It does, but you're already on tape having sex with a married man. We don't want to add any additional negative stigmas."

"Darcy, I appreciate your concern about protecting my reputation, but don't. I could care less if people like or respect me, as long as my name keeps coming out their mouths. Because the more trash they talk the more relevant I become," Lyric stated before pouring herself another glass of champagne. "After craving it for so long, I'm finally getting a taste of being in the spotlight."

Darcy stared at Lyric and wasn't sure if she was the dumbest client she ever had or the smartest. Even her most thirsty-for-fame clients wanted to at least appear to the public that they had some self-respect, even if it was purely for show. Lyric, on the other hand, didn't think it mattered and honestly in a lot of ways she was right. Darcy knew that being a celebrity now wasn't about being loved and respected anymore. It was about staying relevant and it was possible even if people hated everything that person represented. Somehow Lyric had already figured that out which put her ahead of the game.

"We'll do it your way, Lyric. I'll get all the interviews set up. Hope you're enjoying LA because I think you'll be here for a while," Darcy smiled before making her exit.

"You better believe I'm enjoying LA. I think I might be calling this place home," Lyric said out loud, while scrolling through her iPhone to read some more comments about her sex video debut.

When Lyric initially hatched her plan, she had no inkling how she was going to execute it or if it would even work. But she had to give all the credit to Packer since she stole the idea from him. When he confided his plan to teach Cameron a lesson, Lyric decided to use it to her advantage. After she recorded Yaya and Monroe with the basketball player and sent them on their way she decided this was the perfect opportunity to make her debut. Lyric came prepared. She made sure her hair, makeup, matching bra and panty set were all on point. She even tried to get the best lighting possible under the circumstances and had a mount for her iPhone 7plus. She even positioned herself so the camera only captured her best angles.

Lyric went through all that trouble knowing her video might never see the light of day. Luckily for her, the return on investment was high, she had Darcy to partially thank for that. Once Packer told her he wasn't releasing the video of Cameron with Monroe and Yaya, it was time to make her move. Lyric was smart enough to realize she was just the talent with a product to sell, but she needed someone with the business connects to turn her product into some residual income. That's when her Google search on Cameron paid off.

There were tons of articles on him, most glorifying his basketball skills, but the articles regarding Sharon, the wacko who claimed he was her baby daddy, caught Lyric's interest. That's where she came across the name Darcy Woods. The one-time publicist to the stars who had fallen on hard times, due to the slander her one time client Sharon would spew to anyone willing to listen. There was no doubt in Lyric's mind, Darcy was the ideal person for the job and her intuition proved to be correct.

Chapter Twenty-Two

All Alone

"Diamond, please don't leave. We need to talk." Cameron was blocking the bedroom doorway so his wife couldn't leave.

"I'm tired of talking. I feel like we're going in circles. You're not answering any of my questions."

"Because I don't have the answers!" Cameron barked loudly out of frustration. "Yes, that's me on the video and clearly I'm having sex wit' that chick, but I don't know her."

"So, again you're basically telling me you had sex with some random chick and the whole world knows about it. Do you even care how humiliated I am?"

"Baby, of course I care," Cameron said wiping the tears from Diamond's eyes. "This is killing me inside. I would never want to hurt you. I love you and our family more than anything in this world."

"All lies! Love can't possibly hurt this bad. Now please move. I really need some time away from you."

Cameron reluctantly moved out of the way so Diamond could get by. He didn't want to see her go, but knew it was for the best. After she was released from jail a few days earlier, the tension in the house had been almost unbearable. Diamond would scream and yell at Cameron during the day, but then cry herself to sleep at night. With all the obstacles the couple had endured, this seemed to be the turning point in their marriage.

Kennedy hadn't left Sebastian's side once he was moved to a private room after his surgery. She wanted to be the first face Sebastian saw when he came out of his coma. While Kennedy sat in the chair next to his hospital bed, holding Sebastian's hand she saw her phone vibrating on the table.

"Hi, Barry," Kennedy answered in a solemn tone.

"I'm sure you've received my messages, Kennedy."

"I did, but I haven't had the opportunity to speak to anybody. My fiancé was in a horrible car accident a few days ago. I've been at the hospital with him every day and night."

"I'm sorry to hear that, Kennedy, but it doesn't change the fact your payment is past due."

"I know, but I need more time. I was going to get the money from my fiancé, but then he got in that accident and..." Kennedy started to choke up and couldn't finish her sentence.

"I feel terrible for you, I really do and I hope your fiancé pulls through but..."

"He's in a fuckin' coma, Barry!" she sobbed. "You can't seriously be pressing me about this payment right now."

"I told you it's not my money. Honestly, Kennedy this is just a courtesy call."

"What does that mean?"

"The person you got the loan from is going to start legal action to enforce the agreement you signed, so prepare yourself," Barry warned.

"Prepare myself for what... a lawsuit?"

"Probably, but the first thing he's going to take is your company."

"What!" Kennedy let go of Sebastian's hand and took her call to the hallway realizing things were about to get heated. "What the hell are you talking about? Nobody is taking Glitz Inc. That's my company!"

"Read the fine lines, Kennedy. It's all written in your agreement. By the end of the week, you will no longer be the owner of Glitz Inc. I'm sorry," Barry said before hanging up.

Kennedy could feel her hand moving and when she looked down, it was shaking uncontrollably. She placed her other hand over it to make it stop, but it didn't help. She ran into the bathroom, turned on the faucet and started splashing water over her face. Kennedy glanced at her reflection in the mirror. The dark circles only intensified the sadness in her eyes. Between the lack of sleep and not eating, she no longer recognized herself. Kennedy was losing her company and possibly the man that she loved. Her life was on a downward spiral and she didn't know how to get it back on track.

"Do you have anything stronger?" Diamond asked when Blair handed her a glass of freshly squeezed orange juice.

"Sorry. I'm about to start working on a new movie in a few weeks so I'm trying to keep my diet super clean," Blair informed her.

"The last thing I probably need is some liquor. I'm sure I would end up doing something reckless if I'm anything but sober."

"We all saw what a lil' caffeine in your system had you out there doing, so that would be a no on alcohol," Blair joked and they both laughed.

"Thanks for making me laugh. The mood I've been in, I didn't think that was possible," Diamond said, putting her orange juice down on the end table and picking up the newspaper. "What's this?"

"Oh, gosh! I meant to throw that away before you got here." Blair reached to take the paper away from Diamond, but her grip was too tight.

"NBA Superstar Cameron Robinson's wife turns into a madwoman when sex video is released," Diamond read out loud. "Wow, that's some headline. They even have a picture of me smashing my truck into his car," she said, shaking her head.

"Well, at least you made the front page of the New York Post."

"The jokes with you are endless today," Diamond remarked, reading the article, which was full of half truths. "How long do you think this nightmare is gonna last?"

"Honestly, I have no clue. It seems to be gaining momentum because the woman in the video seems hell bent on keeping the story going."

"I know. It's like she's everywhere. I've stopped going online because stories about her keep popping up. I guess she's accomplished her goal of becoming famous," Diamond scoffed. "And can you believe Cameron claims he doesn't even know her or remember when they had sex. The audacity of him."

"I don't know how he can forget. It was the night of that bachelor party he went to with Kirk," Blair stated casually.

"How do you know that?" Diamond asked.

"Know what?"

"When Cameron made that sex video. How do you know it was the night of the Bachelor party?" Diamond sat up straight in the chair and moved her body forward. She was giving Blair a harsh stare.

It wasn't until that very moment did Blair realize she had fucked up. By getting too comfortable and speaking freely, she told on herself.

"Answer the question, Blair!"

"I guess I have no choice, but to tell you the truth." The hesitance in Blair's voice only infuriated Diamond.

"Spit it out!"

"Remember a few months ago when I left Kirk because I saw a video of him having sex with another woman."

"How can I forget," Diamond snapped, wanting Blair to get to the point.

"In that same video, I saw Cameron having sex too and it was the night of that bachelor party."

"So, you already knew about the video that was leaked with him and that woman?"

"No, it was a different video, but I could tell it was filmed in the same bedroom on the same night.

The only difference is the one I saw, he was with two other women at the same time."

"What!" Diamond screamed. Then in a split second, her voice went low and calm before saying, "You saw Cameron in a video having sex with two other women and you never told me."

Diamond's demeanor had Blair feeling uneasy, but Pandora's box had been opened and she had to deal with ramifications. "I wanted to tell you the truth. I almost did, but..."

"But what?! What reason could you possibly have for not telling me that you saw my husband fuckin' two other women... huh, Blair?!" Diamond jumped up and was back to her loud accusatory tone.

"When I came over and told you about Kirk, my intention was to tell you about Cameron too. But Cameron called me on my way over and begged me not to say anything."

"Wait a minute." Diamond put her hand up as if taking a moment to process what she was hearing. "Cameron knew you had seen a video of him having a fuck fest, but kept it from me. Now your Cameron's protector? How many more secrets do you and my husband share?"

"None! Diamond, it wasn't like that. I didn't keep the secret to protect Cameron."

"Then why!"

"For you. I was trying to protect you. When I came over that day, you went on and on about how happy you were with Cameron and you were planning this romantic vacation. I hadn't seen you that happy in so long. I didn't want to kill your joy."

"Kill my joy!" Diamond shook her head with repulsion. "What do you think has happened to me now. My joy is dead," she scoffed. "Gosh," Diamond glanced up at the ceiling rolling her eyes. "I see you're still the same naïve, gullible, dumb girl I always had to protect when we were growing up. Because only a fool would think I'd rather find out my husband cheated on me at the same time as the rest of the world instead of my best friend delivering the blow."

"Diamond, I never knew the video was going to come out and the one that I saw didn't. Skee made sure that it was deleted."

"Skee knew too? Oh gosh." Diamond's eyes watered up and she began biting down on her lip wanting to subdue her anger before it boiled over and she blew up. "Everyone knew my husband was fuckin' around but me. I can expect the deceit from everyone else but you, Blair."

"I'm so sorry. I did feel guilty for not telling you the truth. If I would've thought for one second any version of a sex video with Cameron in it was going to come out, I would've told you the truth."

"It's easy to say that now. You had an opportunity, but instead of easing my humiliation by forewarning me of what was to come, you kept me in the dark. Maybe if I knew ahead of time, I wouldn't have gone all road rage, destroying Cameron's car and getting myself arrested in the process. How could you?"

"Diamond, I told you I was sorry, but let's be real for a second. Hypothetically, if I had told you the truth, what would you have done about it?"

"Excuse me... what sort of question is that?"

"A legit one. When I told you about Kirk's cheating, you were practically begging me to give him another chance."

"And..." Diamond folded her arms becoming defensive.

"You would've found a reason to forgive Cameron and excuse his behavior. You wouldn't have left him or ended your marriage. The only thing I would've accomplished was being the best friend who couldn't mind her business and the deliverer of bad news."

"You don't know what I would've done. You denied giving me the choice by keeping what you knew to yourself."

"Okay, so now you know, Diamond. What are you going to do with the information... are you leaving Cameron?"

The women appeared to be having a standoff on who could remain silent the longest. Blair continued waiting for an answer to her question, but got nothing. Instead, Diamond was full of rage and it all seemed to be directed at her best friend.

"What happens in my life is no longer any of your business," Diamond finally spoke up and said, then grabbed her purse off the sofa. "You're obviously not the friend I thought you were and I don't need you in my life."

"Wait! After everything we've been through together, you're going to end our friendship over this?!" Now Blair was glaring at Diamond with the same rage she had been the recipient of.

"Clearly this friendship was one-sided because I would've never done this to you. I don't want someone in my life that I don't trust. You should understand since that's the very reason you cut Kennedy out of yours."

"The difference is, I was looking out for your wellbeing by keeping what I knew to myself, Kennedy was looking out for herself. I don't even know how you can compare the two. But who cares," Blair snapped, walking over and opening the front door. "If you want to throw away our friendship over this, then I don't need you either!"

"Fine!" Diamond shot back and walked out.

Blair slammed the door behind her, then sat down on her sofa before bursting out in tears. She was filled with a combination of sadness and anger over the devastation of losing her best friend. Without Diamond and Kennedy in her life, she was beginning to feel completely alone.

Chapter Twenty-Three

Bye Bye Baby

Packer had watched the sex video of Cameron and Lyric numerous times, but the blow to his ego never softened. He felt stupid that he got played by who he considered to be nothing more than an Instagram booty model. Now he was left wondering how he could've been so clueless. So, for the last few weeks, Packer constantly replayed the last conversation he had with Lyric to figure out where he went wrong.

"You goin' on a trip?" Packer had laughed when he got home and saw Lyric in a tank top with boy shorts packing a suitcase.

"If I am, why would you find that funny?" Lyric had asked.

"I mean it ain't like you can afford to really go any place without me. You ain't got no real money." He smiled. "Since I ain't planned no trips, I was making a joke. That's all."

"Ha... ha... ha! That's me laughing at your so-called joke," Lyric had said as she continued to pack her suitcase.

"What's up wit' the suitcase?"

"I know it's farfetched to think I can afford a plane ticket to leave the state of New York without you, but stranger things have happened," Lyric had replied sarcastically, stuffing one last pair of shoes in her suitcase then zipping it up.

Packer had watched Lyric take off her boy shorts and squeeze into some super tight high-waisted jeans that amplified every curve on her lower body. She then slipped on some pointed toe, gold clear mules with Lucite heels. She had fluffed out her fresh weave, applied some lip gloss and put on some hoop earrings.

"I don't know what type of game you playin' or point you tryna make, but you can stop this bullshit. You still mad I didn't take you shoppin' last week? Man, I done got you so fuckin' spoiled," Packer had cracked.

"I would stay and entertain this conversation, but I have a flight to LA I need to catch." Lyric grabbed her large carry-on and suitcase.

"LA! You 'bout to catch a flight to LA... for what?"

"Business."

"You ain't got no business in LA. You goin' to see some other nigga," he accused, grabbing her arm.

"Let go of my arm!" Lyric had barked, snatching her arm loose.

"Whatever! Take yo' ass to LA, but you'll be crawling back. 'Cause like I said. I got yo' ass spoiled. Niggas ain't out here spendin' money on pussy like that no mo'. You betta hope when you come back, I ain't already replaced yo' ass," Packer had scoffed.

Lyric didn't acknowledge a single word Packer had spit. She simply continued out the door with her belongings. At the time Packer hadn't been worried though. He figured Lyric was having one of her temper tantrums and would come right back and they would fuck and make up. But a day had passed, then another day, and on the third day was when the sex video hit the Internet and Packer felt like the biggest loser. The crazy part was he was more furious with Cameron than he was at Lyric. The video only fueled Packer's desire, even more, to wreak havoc on the Superstar NBA Player's life.

Kennedy woke up Monday afternoon to ten missed

calls from Tammy and three text messages. She had only been in the office once since Sebastian's car accident and assumed her longtime assistant was probably feeling overwhelmed.

"Let me call Tammy back and let her know I'm coming in today," Kennedy said out loud, hitting her name on the recent call log.

"Finally! Girl, I been blowing you up all morning," Tammy said when she answered the phone after the first ring.

"Last night was the first time I got any real sleep. I guess I got a little carried away. What's going on?" Kennedy was still trying to drag herself out of bed. With fatigue and worrying about Sebastian's recovery, being in the bed was the only place Kennedy wanted to be.

"Did you change the lock on the door?"

"No!"

"Well somebody did because my key is not working."

"Are you sure?"

"Positive. This the same key I been using. It worked just fine when I came to work Friday, but come Monday, it ain't opening the door," Tammy hissed.

"Where are you now?"

"I came to that Starbucks down the street from the office. I'm using their Wi-Fi to conduct company business. So, what's up with the locks?"

"Not sure," Kennedy lied. "I'ma find out what's going on and I'll be to you within the hour so stay put."

When Kennedy ended the call with Tammy, she collapsed right back down in the bed. She stared up at the ceiling in complete dismay. Kennedy dreaded to make the next phone call, but knew she had no choice.

"Good afternoon, Kennedy. I was expecting to hear from you early this morning," Barry said, leaning back in his chair.

"You can't possibly be this cold-blooded. I told you my fiancé was in a coma and he still is. Please tell me you're not responsible for having the locks changed at my office." Kennedy was seething, but held out on wishing death upon Barry until she heard what he had to say.

"I didn't have your locks changed, but the new owner did. When we spoke over a week ago, I made it clear you defaulted on the loan and the lender would be taking over your business which he has every legal right to do," Barry explained.

"How in the hell did he pull this off so fast and there is no way it can be legal!" Kennedy scoffed.

"Read the agreement you signed. It's all legal. Your lender is an attorney, so he would know."

"Who is this fuckin' lender?!" Kennedy shouted.

"Brimstone Holding Group. It's right there in your paperwork."

"I don't want the name of some bullshit dummy company. I want the owner's government name."

"I'm unable to give you that information. The lender wishes to remain anonymous which is also within his legal rights."

"Barry, why do I have the strong suspicion that I'm being fucked and not only are you aware of this, but you also played a major role in making it happen."

"Kennedy, you came to me for a favor and I helped you out. Don't blame me because you were unable to sustain your end of the agreement and lost your company in the process. I have another call, but take care of yourself."

Barry's dismissive attitude was all the motivation Kennedy needed to hop out of bed, take a quick shower, throw some clothes on and head to her office. She wanted to know who was the conniving sonofabitch who managed to steal Glitz Inc. from right under her nose.

"Man, I need to learn how to play poker," Kirk told Cameron while they were leaving out the gambling spot in Harlem. "I'm tired of coming wit' you and being a bystander," he complained.

"I feel you. Just know once you catch the gambling bug, ain't no turning back," Cameron warned. "You ready for that?"

"Mos def. I got a couple mil' I can play wit'," Kirk said smirking.

"Watch what you say 'cause you can lose a few million real quick when it come to this gambling shit. I need to slow down my damn self," Cameron admitted, thinking about all the money that had slipped through is fingers due to his gambling fixation.

"I hear you, man." Kirk laughed, noticing a familiar face walking in their direction.

"We left right on time," Cameron mumbled to Kirk.

"Where you think you goin'," Packer said to Cameron in a friendly voice. "It's been a long time since we've met at the poker table. I think we need to catch up."

"Sorry, man, can't do that." Cameron smiled, hitting the unlock button on his car remote. "I've already played. Maybe next time."

"Yeah, maybe." Packer nodded in a condescending way. "I see you've replaced that Lambo yo' girl went ham on," he remarked, looking over at Cameron's car. "You need to treat wifey better next time, so you don't have those types of problems."

"Don't speak on my wife." Cameron's jaw began flinching. It was one thing for Packer to make snide remarks regarding gambling, but his family was off limits.

"Now she's yo' wife. Was she yo' wife when you was fuckin' my girl Lyric on that sex video... huh?"

"What tha fuck! Yo' girl? I don't even know that broad and like I said, don't speak on my wife." Cameron was now standing in Packer's face. They were so close they could hear each other breathing. Two of Packer's boys ran up, lifting their shirts to show they were carrying heat.

"We good over here." Packer put his hand up letting his boys know to simmer down.

"Come on. You don't need this, man," Kirk said grabbing on Cameron's arm to pull him away.

"You need to listen to yo' boy," Packer suggested.

"Don't you have a poker game or something to play," Kirk frowned, eyeing Packer. "Let's go, Cameron. He ain't worth it."

Cameron was pissed and ready to punch Packer in his mouth, but took Kirk's advice and walked away. "That motherfucker got a lot of nerves." Cameron slammed his car door and was steaming.

"Fuck him!" Kirk said as Packer and his cronies continued to stare them down from the sidewalk.

"And what the fuck did he mean his girl? So the chick on that video I was in, is Packer's girlfriend?

That don't even make no sense," Cameron said driving off.

"Don't nothing that nigga say make any sense. Pay him no mind. He all talk and no bark. Now let's go eat." Kirk forgot about Packer the moment he was out of his eyesight, but it wasn't that easy for Cameron. He had a bad feeling no matter how hard he tried to shake it.

Chapter Twenty-Four

That's When I Knew

Kennedy arrived at what used to be her office in search of answers. The locks were changed as Tammy said, but Kennedy still had paperwork showing she was the owner of the building. She used that paperwork to get a commercial locksmith to gain her access into the office by claiming she had lost her keys.

"Thank you so much!" Kennedy said politely to the locksmith. She handed over the cash and hurried him along so she could do some snooping around. Kennedy was determined to find out who was the new owner of Glitz Inc. She reasoned if she could talk to this mystery lender herself, she could somehow convince him to give her more time and get her company back.

"Everything looks the same," Kennedy commented out loud while looking around. She started to doubt she would find anything pointing in the direction of the new owner since it looked exactly how she left it. Kennedy then spotted a navy 12-pocket stadium file on one of the desks. She had never seen it before.

"This has to belong to the new owner," Kennedy mumbled looking through the folder labeled clients.

"Who are you?"

Kennedy was completely startled by the loud voice she almost knocked over the files. She glanced up and saw a curvy woman who seemed tastelessly dressed for an early Monday afternoon in a spandex, deep sage crop top with a matching mini skirt and six-inch heels staring at her.

"This is my office. Who are you and why are you here?" Kennedy grilled.

"My name is Lyric and this isn't your office." She shook her head thinking Kennedy resembled a bike messenger in her sweats, t-shirt, Nike shoes, and baseball cap. "The *real* owner," Lyric stressed, "left something in her car and will be back any second."

"Her?" Kennedy questioned remembering that Barry always referred to the lender as a man.

"Yes! And her name is..." before Lyric could get the name out, Darcy came strolling in with her oversized matte black sunglasses.

"What do we have here!" Darcy beamed.

"I caught this woman in—"

"Darcy, what in the hell are you doing here?!" Kennedy screamed cutting Lyric off and rushing past her towards her nemesis.

"I think you better calm down, Kennedy, before I call the police and have you arrested for trespassing," Darcy smirked.

"There is no way you're the owner of this office building. I doubt you even have a hundred dollars to your name," Kennedy snapped.

"That's where you're wrong. Business is now booming."

"That's right!" Lyric chimed in. "I'm her new client and now that money is steady flowing." Lyric bragged, clapping her hands like she was hot shit.

"I don't know what type of client you are, but I can guarantee you're not bringing in the type of money Darcy would need to pull this stunt off," Kennedy huffed, wishing this Lyric chick would shut the fuck up and go away.

"None of that matters, Kennedy. Glitz Inc. is now mine. How I pulled it off is a moot point. You should've never crossed me. Don't embarrass yourself any further by not only losing your company, but walking out of here in handcuffs."

"You're enjoying this." Kennedy bit down on her lip to calm her nerves. Her anger had her ready to cry, fight, and shred shit up, but common sense prevailed.

"I wasn't planning on having you find out like this. But I must admit, yes, I'm taking great pleasure watching your world crumble right before your eyes. How does it feel to have nothing, Kennedy?"

"It would be easy for me to drag yo' ass across this floor, but that would only bring me momentary satisfaction. Enjoy this temporary win, Darcy, because that's what it is." Kennedy then proceeded to start grabbing things from around the office she wanted to take with her.

"You can't take that stuff!" Lyric shouted at Kennedy. "Are you gonna let her get away wit' this, Darcy?!"

"Stay in your lane!" Kennedy barked at Lyric. "Darcy is an evil, trifling skank, but she ain't stupid. Stopping me from getting my belongings would be a huge mistake."

"Don't worry about it, Lyric. There's nothing else Kennedy has that I want. Whatever she doesn't take is going in the trash anyway."

Kennedy began counting down the days she would be able to smack that smug look off Darcy's face. Until then she would have to figure out what her next move would be.

"Blair, you have another flower delivery. They've been coming nonstop for what, two weeks now," the production assistant on the movie set said coming into her dressing room.

"They're beautiful." Blair smiled putting them on the table.

"It looks like Skee isn't giving up anytime soon especially since he's waiting outside to talk to you."

"Are you serious! Tell him to come in." Blair leaned over and smelled the ombre roses.

"I take it you like the flowers." Skee grinned walking over and giving Blair a kiss on the cheek.

"Who wouldn't, they're beautiful. If you send me any more, I'll be able to open up my own floral shop."

"Then get ready to open that shop, cause I'ma keep sending you flowers until you have dinner with me."

"Skee, I told you I'm not ready to start dating yet. I'm focusing on my career. After I finish filming this Indie film, I'm headed to LA to start working on another movie. I don't need any distractions."

"I respect the fact you're dedicated to your career. I think it's sexy. Can I be your date when you attend the Oscars and win," Skee said smiling, wrapping his arms around Blair's waist.

"Stop playing with me." Blair playfully pounded on Skee's chest. "I doubt an Oscar is anywhere in my future."

"You gotta think big, Blair. Whatever you want, you must visualize it, believe it can and will happen. Just like I want you." Skee stroked the side of Blair's face. "All I'm asking is for one dinner date… please."

"Okay, but it can't be until Friday."

"I can do Friday."

"There's one other stipulation."

"Name it."

"I still expect for these beautiful flowers to be delivered every day. Do we have a deal?" Blair had a glimmer in her eyes.

"That's one deal I have no problem agreeing to. I do have one request of my own." Skee held up his index finger.

"What is it?"

"I've missed those lips. Can I get a kiss?"

Instead of Blair answering the question, she leaned forward. Their lips and tongue became one. The kiss was lingering and intense. Even after so much time had passed, their chemistry was undeniable.

"Damn. Now I realize why I missed your lips so much."

"I can't deny it. Kissing you felt right."

"Because it is right. You need to stop being stubborn and give a nigga another chance. I won't fuck up again. I promise."

"I wanna believe you but between Kirk, Kennedy, and now Diamond, who I never thought

I would stop being friends with, my trust factor is on zero."

"You still haven't spoken to Diamond?"

"Nope. But I did read in the paper they dropped the criminal charges against her which I'm happy about."

"She did only damage her car and Cameron's and I'm positive he wasn't pressing no charges, so I can see them dropping the criminal charges."

"Yeah, that does make sense. Their marriage doesn't need any more stress, so hopefully it works out although it's no longer my concern," Blair shrugged, sitting down in the chair to check her hair and makeup before going back on set.

"I know how much you care about Diamond." Skee rested his hands on Blair's shoulders and began to gently massage them. "In time, you all will make up and be best friends again."

"The more time goes by, the more unlikely that becomes, but I'm cool with it. People change and friendships grow apart. I wish Diamond well, but she's out of my life and I'm moving forward with mine," Blair stated with no regrets.

"You ain't got nothing to worry about 'cause you got me and I'm not going nowhere."

Blair laid her hand on top of Skee's. The warmth from his body eased her mind. His presence brought her comfort and a feeling of security she hadn't felt in a very long time. Blair began to contemplate having a future with Skee might be in the cards.

"Diamond, I've been staying in a hotel for weeks. I was trying to give you space, but I need to know, is this gonna be permanent?"

Diamond was putting some clothes away in Elijah's room when Cameron came in. She wasn't in the mood to discuss the future of their marriage. But it was evident by her husband's demeanor, he wanted answers and trying to avoid the conversation wasn't going to make Cameron go away.

"I never told you to go stay in a hotel," Diamond replied flatly, continuing to put away her son's clothes, not looking at Cameron. She was slick trying to dance around giving him a straight answer to his question.

"I didn't have much of a choice. You were barely speakin' to me. We weren't even sleeping in the same bed. I felt like a stranger in my own damn house."

"Whose fault is that!" she shouted, now making eye contact with her husband. You're the one who embarrassed me in front of the entire fuckin' world because you couldn't keep your dick in your pants!"

"You neva gonna let me forget that shit." Cameron pounded his fist on the wall and shook his head in frustration. "I told you I was sorry. What more can I do?"

"Give me time. This shit is still fresh in my mind."

"That's what I wanna know. How much time do you need? Do I need to start looking for my own place because I can't keep living that hotel life," Cameron stated.

"Finding your own place might be for the best. This ain't no happy home and I have no idea if it will ever be again."

Diamond immediately saw the despair in Cameron's eyes after she spoke her truth. In her heart, the love Diamond had for her husband hadn't changed, but the pain and anger ran equally as deep. For them to be together now would only cause more resentment instead of healing a broken marriage.

Chapter Twenty-Five

The Present....

"Are you ready for tonight?" Skee turned to Blair and asked, leaning back in the limo.

"No," Blair admitted, taking another sip of her champagne to help ease her anxiety. "If you would've told me a year ago I would be attending the Met Gala, I never would've believed it."

"Believe it, baby!" Skee winked. "Now that Oscar don't seem so unobtainable... does it?"

"One goal at a time. I'm not ready to wrap my mind around an Oscar just yet."

"You got rave reviews at Sundance for that Independent movie you did and next month you have the movie coming out wit' Idris Elba and Ryan

Reynolds. You big time now." Skee grinned widely.

"I'm not big time yet, but thanks for the vote of confidence. How lucky am I that my boyfriend is my biggest cheerleader."

"I'm the lucky one." Skee slid his hand up Blair's toned, bare legs. "The giant slash cut down the front makes for easy access. I can dig that."

"Stop it!" Blair patted Skee's hand away. "It took me forever to get in this heavy ass couture La Perla gown. All this sparkly crystal mesh is great to look at, but it ain't no fun to wear."

Skee placed a few kisses on Blair's inner thigh then stopped. "Because you need to be photo ready when we hit the red carpet. We'll continue this when we get back to the crib," he said kissing her thigh one last time. "It's show time, baby."

The limo came to a standstill so Blair finished the last of the champagne. She studied her reflection in the mirror, quickly reapplying some lipstick and closed her eyes. When she opened them, the driver had the door ajar and the song "Flashing Lights" played in her head as Blair stepped out the limo like she owned the Met Gala.

"Look at this bitch," Monroe smacked, staring at Lyric on the television screen. "Like is she seriously on this season of Basketball Wives. Who knew all you had to do was fuck a NBA star and you instantly qualified to be on this show."

"If that's the case, then I need to be on that show too as many NBA niggas I done ran through," Yaya chimed in.

"Well none of us were smart enough to make a video fuckin' one of those NBA niggas and releasing that shit. Lyric damn sure parlaying the hell out this shit. Can't knock her fuckin' hustle," Taj said, shrugging. "I'm just mad I didn't think of that shit."

"Now I see why she changed her number and got ghost." Monroe folded her arms pissed. "Fuck her! Turn that shit off." Monroe grabbed the television remote off the table and hit the power button.

"I don't think that's why she changed her number," Yaya spoke up and said.

"Why you say that... have you spoken to her?" Taj questioned.

"No, but a few weeks ago I ran into Packer up in Harlem. He was grilling me about Lyric. All that shit popped off over a year ago and that nigga still out for blood. I think he's the reason Lyric changed her number, cause Packer fuckin' harassing her," Yaya reasoned.

"Packer mad cause he got played. He figured he was dealing wit' a dumb ho happy he was spending some coins. Little did he know Lyric had much bigger ideas!" Taj burst out laughing. "I'm imagining how sick that nigga felt when he saw the dude he paid the two of you to set up, dicking down his girl."

"Oh, now you know that motherfucker was hot!" Monroe laughed. "I'm hot my fuckin' self. We stuck in NYC barely making ends meet while Lyric over in LA making major moves. We all used to run tricks on niggas together, like why she ain't bring us to LA wit' her. If it wasn't for us, she wouldn't even have had an opportunity to make that sex video. Yo, she foul."

"I still got love for Lyric and it's nice seeing one of us make it, but you do have a point, Monroe," Yaya agreed. "We all homegirls. If I got put on, I would def put my girls on too. It's like Lyric used us and then cut us off once she didn't need us no more."

"Don't none of that shit matter," Taj said, playing with the tips of her auburn hair. "I mean Lyric found a way to get her come up. We can either sit here in this cramped apartment and complain or we can figure out how to get our own come up."

The women all looked at each other while sitting on the cold hardwood floor pondering what Taj said. Coming up with a scheme was always the easy part, executing said scheme into a major come up was the hard part. But watching Lyric pull it off effortlessly gave Monroe, Yaya, and Taj the boost of confidence they needed.

"It's not too late for us to have Elijah's birthday party at the Children's Museum. I never cancelled the reservations," Diamond informed her mother.

"Why are you being difficult? I told you I wanted to have my grandson's birthday party here. The park is right across the street that Elijah loves. Plus, he has a lot of relatives here in Queens that don't like going into the city. Having it here, basically in my front yard makes it convenient for everyone."

"Ma, I'm not trying to make it difficult. I just—"

"You just done got used to living around all that luxury!" Mrs. O'Toole jumped in and said. "You don't think this neighborhood is fancy enough no more. Remember baby girl, this the same house and neighborhood you was born and raised in. This where both you and my first grandbaby Destiny lived too at one time. Don't ever forget where you came from," she said tossing down the dishcloth and walking out the kitchen.

"Don't be like that!" Diamond called out following behind her mother. "I know where I came from. Hell, I might be coming back if Cameron plays hardball in our divorce proceedings. I guess I did visualize a fancy birthday party for Elijah, but you're his grandmother and I know he would enjoy being around his cousins and the rest of our family."

"Of course he would enjoy it. He's a child, Diamond. That boy don't know the difference between some fancy birthday party in the city or one right here at a park across the street. All he wanna do is play, eat cake, and have fun. It's the grownups that be filling their heads with all that materialistic bullshit." She frowned, shaking her head.

"I'll cancel the reservation at the Children's Museum and start making preparations to have the party here. We have plenty of time to plan it. His birthday isn't for a few more months. Okay?"

"Good. I'll let the family know. They'll be so happy to see you, Diamond." Mrs. O'Toole couldn't help but notice her daughter turning away and putting her head down. "Baby girl, are you alright... are you that upset about the party?"

"No, Ma." Diamond let out a slight giggle. "I'm over the whole pricey birthday party. The most important thing is Elijah being with his family and he will be."

"Then what got you over there looking so depressed?"

"I guess the idea of being around family members I haven't seen in a few years isn't something I'm looking forward to," Diamond disclosed.

"Why? These are people you grew up with and love you."

"They're also the same people I'm sure know all about my pending divorce and what led up to it.

Especially now that the woman in the center of it all is starting in a reality show I bet they watch. It's all so embarrassing. When will it stop."

"It will stop once you say no more. You don't have to explain your marriage to nobody. That's between you and your husband. When you allow other folks to dictate what your marital status needs to be, you asking to forever be single."

"I hear you, but it doesn't make the humiliation or the process of going through a public divorce any easier."

"I'm sure that's true, but get yourself a hobby and focus on your kids. They should keep you so busy and wore out that you'll be too tired to worry about all that foolishness. Go have some drinks with Blair," she suggested. "That's what friends are for."

"You know Blair and I fell out," Diamond reminded her mother.

"You still ain't talking to Blair?!" Mrs. O'Toole placed her hand on her hip, surprised by what she heard. "I just knew you all had made up by now. I figured I would see her and that cute lil' son of hers at Elijah's party."

"I wanted to invite her, but she changed her phone number. A few months ago, I reached out to her and it was disconnected."

"And she hasn't tried calling you?"

"Nope. I even relayed a message through Kirk for her to call me, but she never responded."

"I can't blame her." Mrs. O'Toole walked over to a bookshelf in the living room and picked up a picture. "You and Blair were always so close," she said, looking at their picture. "You were like sisters."

"That's why I can't believe she kept a secret of such magnitude from me," Diamond said, still harboring anger over what happened.

"Didn't I just tell you what goes on in your marriage is between you and your husband. I'm sure Blair felt compelled to tell you what she knew, but that girl did what more people need to do... mind they business."

"I don't agree with that, but I do think ending my friendship with Blair was a huge mistake. One I might regret for the rest of my life since it seems she wants nothing to do with me. I've lost my husband and my best friend."

"Are you going to invite Cameron to Elijah's birthday party?"

"What kind of question is that? He's Elijah's father, of course I'm inviting him."

"I don't know why you're acting shocked I asked the question. You practically pushed Cameron to file for divorce. I could see you not wanting him to come."

"Are you really blaming me for our marriage ending? Cameron is the one who cheated! Not only that, his sex video will forever live in cyber world!" Diamond yelled.

"Now you know I wanted to smack the shit out that boy when I saw on the news you were arrested and then learned what he did to send you over the edge. That man broke my baby's heart and I was furious. But Cameron did everything he could to win you back and keep his family together. That wasn't enough for you. You wouldn't let go of your anger. You're still holding on to it and that's why you lost your husband."

"No! I lost my husband because he screwed some hussy and his dumbass let her record it. So, excuse me if I can't erase those visuals out of my mind and simply forgive and forget. Now let's just agree to disagree because I'm over this conversation," Diamond scoffed grabbing her car keys. "I need to go pick up Destiny. I'll call you later so I can make sure we start getting everything coordinated for Elijah's birthday party."

Diamond rushed out her mother's house full of rage and sadness. What her mother or no one else understood was that she did want to save her marriage. Being without Cameron made her physically sick. There were some days when Diamond couldn't get out of bed because she yearned for her husband. But the wrath of a woman scorned would not allow Diamond to let down her wall and allow her husband back in.

"Kennedy, do you have that report for me on our new client?"

"I'm printing it out for you now, Mr. Weiner," she said smiling.

"Good. Bring it to my office once you're done."

Kennedy turned around in her chair and rolled her eyes when he left her office. Although she was hired as a senior account executive at the high-powered Public Relations firm, she was no more than a glorified secretary for her boss, Mr. Weiner. The only good thing about the job was the pay. Kennedy had no creative input and it was driving her crazy. She missed her days of running Glitz Inc. even when the business was struggling financially. At least it was her company and she had control over whether it flourished or failed. Those days were now over, but Kennedy hadn't given up on her dream of getting it back. For now, those aspirations had been put on hold.

A lot had changed in the past year. After Sebastian's car accident, it took him months to get better. It wasn't until recently he was able to go back to work, running his business full time. They were financially strapped for cash, so when Kennedy was offered this position, she couldn't say no. Plus, the job description sounded enticing, unfortunately, it was only on paper. Now Kennedy was stuck doing mediocre tasks for a check.

Kennedy retrieved the papers she printed and scanned through them one more time before giving the report to Mr. Weiner. On her way to his office, she recognized a very familiar face. *Isn't that the woman who was with Darcy at my office? Her taste in clothes has gotten better, but I would never forget that face,* Kennedy thought to herself.

"Hey, Brad! How's it going?" Kennedy didn't typically socialize much at the office, but she knew how to work it whenever she wanted to.

"Everything is going great. I'm about to head out to lunch, care to join me?"

"I would, but I have to go over this report with Mr. Weiner," she said holding up the papers. "But maybe next time. That woman I just saw leaving your office," Kennedy smoothly transitioned to the next subject. "I feel like I've seen her somewhere before."

"Oh, that was Lyric Nunez. You probably seen her on that reality show... what's the name of it?" Brad snapped his finger trying to remember. "You know the basketball show."

"Basketball Wives on VH1?"

"Yes! That's the one."

"What basketball player is she married to?"

"None. She got her fame the Kim Kardashian way. A sex video with Cameron Robinson."

Kennedy had to stop herself from choking when Brad told her that. "When was this?"

"A year or so ago, I think."

Kennedy wondered how she missed something that explosive, but it must've been during the time when Sebastian was in the hospital and she cut herself off from work, social media, basically everything. She immediately thought about Diamond, hoping she was okay. They hadn't spoken in over a year. Their friendship ended at the same time Blair wanted nothing to do with her.

"So, what did this Lyric woman want with you?"

"She's trying to clean up her image. Put the whole sex video thing behind her."

"I'm surprised she doesn't already have a PR rep," Kennedy commented remembering Darcy said Lyric was her client when they had their confrontation at her office.

"From my understanding, Darcy Woods was representing her, but she recently severed their relationship. Now Ms. Nunez is looking for an agency that can take her career to the next level and who better than our firm."

"Does that mean she's going to become a client?"

"Yep! That's why she stopped by my office, to sign the agreement. Watch me turn her image from trashy to classy," Brad boasted. "You know if anybody can work a miracle, it's me."

"No doubt." Kennedy smiled. "Listen, I better get to Mr. Weiner's office. You know he doesn't like to be kept waiting."

"Of course, and don't forget you owe me a lunch date." Brad winked and headed down the hall.

So, Lyric is our new client. This should be very interesting. I'm sure she has a lot of information regarding Darcy and with any luck some juicy dirt. I'll have to figure out how to use that to my advantage, Kennedy thought to herself before going into her boss's office.

Chapter Twenty-Six

Shots Fired

"Ma, the park looks great!" Diamond gushed when she and Destiny arrived.

"Yes! I love it, grandma!" Destiny's eyes gleamed, hugging her grandmother. "I'll be back. I'm going to play," she said running off towards the playground to join the other kids.

"Everything really does look perfect. I love the whole robots and rockets theme," Diamond added.

"Those are the two things my grandson seems to be obsessed with right now. I figured he would love it. I even did the cake in the shape of a robot." She smiled showing Diamond.

"He's going to go crazy. I can't wait for Elijah to

see it. That robot cake looks amazing! What bakery did you use?"

"Grandma O'Toole's bakery. That's who."

"You baked that cake yourself?!"

"Yes! Why you acting so surprised? Yo' mama could always cook."

"Who you telling! Don't I stay begging you to make my favorite meals? But I had no idea you could create fancy cakes like this. Girl, you need to open up a bakery."

"Chile, please." Diamond's mom waved her hand, dismissing what her daughter said as a joke.

"I'm serious! Not only can you cook but you got skills. Bakeries charge big money for cakes like this. Think about it."

"Who gonna pay for this so-called bakery... huh?"

"Cameron and I talked about the divorce the other day and from what he said, he's going to give me a pretty decent settlement."

"I knew he would."

"I wasn't sure. I did sign a prenup, so it could've went either way."

"Cameron has his flaws, but he loves Elijah and Destiny. He also loves you. I knew he would be fair with the divorce settlement."

"Well, once it's all resolved, I should have more than enough to open up a bakery for you," Diamond winked.

"Are you serious? You wanna open up a bakery for yo' mama?" Mrs. O'Toole put her hand on her hip and leaned back not believing what she was hearing.

"I truly do. I think you would do great. Is it something you would be interested in doing?"

"Would I.... of course! I never fixed my mind to believe it would be possible. I'm not even gonna let myself get excited until you give me the green light."

"I'm giving you the green light. When my divorce is finalized, we're opening a bakery. Helping you with this will also keep me busy and my mind off the divorce."

"I can't believe my baby girl is doing this for me. Thank you!" she reached over and gave Diamond a huge hug. "I feel like it's my birthday too."

"It makes me feel good to see you so happy. Honestly, I'm thrilled about it too. This is going to be amazing."

"I agree. The perfect mother and daughter venture. Wait until I tell my grandchildren. Speaking of them, what time is Elijah coming? Everybody is here, but the birthday boy."

"Cameron had something planned for him earlier today. He sent me a text saying they were finishing up and they would be here shortly," Diamond explained.

"Good, because the way these kids playing so hard, I know they ready for some cake and ice cream," Mrs. O'Toole commented, glancing over, seeing Destiny running around with the other little kids playing tag. "Watching the kids have all that fun warms my heart. Your uncle even brought some firecrackers. The kids will go crazy over that. This is going to be the best birthday party ever. A day I'll remember for the rest of my life," Mrs. O'Toole beamed.

Kennedy was dumbfounded at how in the few short months Brad was handling Lyric's account, he was staying true to his word. After a thorough google search, it was easy for Kennedy to see why Lyric needed help cleaning up her image. Darcy had done an excellent job getting her name and likeness out there, but it was strictly on some low level, sex object shit. Based off that, Kennedy didn't have much hope that anything could be done to salvage her reputation, but Brad was making them all believers.

He made one strategic move after another. It was amazing watching what having a major PR firm in your corner could do. Kennedy was no longer annoyed by her job because she was learning invaluable lessons that she would take with her once she got Glitz Inc. back. Brad's first strategic move was to get Lyric an interview and two-page layout in People Magazine. It was a total fluff piece that portrayed her as the misunderstood thot who was over partying and dating different men. She blamed her past behavior with men due to a broken relationship with her father and a mother who was never around to raise her so she had to raise herself.

We had all heard some version of this sad hooker story numerous times, but it never got old because it continuously seemed to work. Like the saying goes, if it ain't broke don't fix it. Brad took Lyric's story and put his own spin on it. He spun it and spun it until he couldn't spin it anymore and the media ate it up. He then had Lyric on the talk show circuit spinning that same sad story. Brad made sure a stylist had her completely covered up in designer clothes that a high-powered attorney would wear instead of the typical ratchet reality show/sex video star attire. Lyric even went from six bundles of twenty-inch Malaysian body wave weave to three bundles and sixteen inches.

Knock... knock... knock...

At first, Kennedy didn't even hear the knocking on her office door because she was in such deep thought, but the persistence eventually got her attention.

"Come in!"

"Kennedy, do you have a minute?" Brad asked stepping inside her office.

"Sure. What can I do for you?"

"I have to take an important meeting with one of our major clients, but I set up a photo shoot and interview for our client, Lyric Nunez. I don't trust her to go alone. She's still rough around the edges. I know you have more important things to do than be a babysitter but..."

"No problem!" she cut in and said. "I'll be more than happy to help you out."

"I like you, Kennedy. You're a team player." Brad winked. "The car will be downstairs in twenty minutes. After the driver picks you up, he'll get Lyric and then take the two of you to the destination. I'll email you over all the details and the point person for the interview. If you have any problems, don't hesitate to call me."

"Thank you, but we'll be fine. I'll make sure Lyric is comfortable and that she gives a great interview." Kennedy smiled.

"I knew I could count on you," Brad said before closing the door.

Yes, you can. I'm looking forward to babysitting Lyric more than you know, Kennedy thought to herself.

"Thank you for inviting me to Elijah's birthday party.

I know things are tense between us right now, but I think it's good for our son to see us together and getting along," Cameron stated.

"I agree," Diamond said nodding. "I want to make this divorce as easy as possible for Elijah and Destiny."

"Mommy... mommy! It's time to open the presents and eat cake!" Elijah ran up to them and said.

"Yes, it is!" Diamond smiled excitedly, picking Elijah up and giving him a kiss.

"Diamond, while I cut that cake can you go across the street to the house and get a present for me. I left the main gift I got for my grandbaby on the living room table," Mrs. O'Toole said.

"Sure. I'll be right back," Diamond said handing Elijah to her mother.

"Thank you, baby girl!"

"It's the least I can do. I mean you basically put this entire party together by yourself. You're the best mom and grandma," Diamond enthused, kissing her mother on the cheek. "Make sure you all save a piece a cake for me!" Diamond called out as she headed to her mother's house.

"Seeing you here with Diamond and the kids makes this day perfect, Cameron," Mrs. O'Toole said warmly to her son-in-law as they watched Diamond going inside the house.

"It feels right. Diamond is still my family."

"She might not admit it, but I know that girl still love you. Fight for your family, Cameron. My daughter and grandbabies need you."

Those were the last words Diamond's mother ever spoke as a hail of gunfire descended upon the once lively birthday party. Pandemonium broke out as the children and their parents all ran and ducked trying to avoid being hit by a bullet. Who would have ever thought that a beautiful, sunny, Saturday afternoon celebration would turn into a bloodbath? As rapid as the barrage of bullets erupted, it came to a halt just as abruptly.

The park filled with silence. No one wanted to move, afraid that the gunfire would commence again at any moment. When Diamond finally came out her mother's house and headed back towards the park, she immediately noticed the mood in the air was different. The cheerful aura now felt dark and depressing.

"What's going on?!" Diamond's voice was full of fear from the unknown. There were people under the picnic tables and behind trees like they were hiding. When they heard her voice, one by one they began lifting their heads and looking up.

"Ma! Destiny! Elijah! Cameron!" she screamed, not seeing any of their faces among the crowd.

"Somebody call 911, my brother's been shot!"

one of the partygoers shouted. That's when Diamond lost it. She ran in the direction where she had left her mother standing with Elijah and Cameron.

Diamond saw Cameron lifting his body from over Elijah and his mother. She ran over to them and almost had a heart attack when she noticed blood on Elijah's shirt. He was crying uncontrollably. Cameron was careful to turn his body over and take him out of Mrs. O'Toole's arms, thinking he had been injured. She had been holding her grandson tightly.

"My baby! My baby... is he okay?!" Diamond cried out.

Cameron lifted Elijah's shirt and didn't see any gunshots. That's when he and Diamond looked down at her mother. She appeared to be so peaceful, too peaceful.

Diamond kneeled on the grass, "Ma... Ma... Ma... say something," she said in a low voice as if she knew there would be no response.

"Mommy! Mommy! What happened?" Destiny finally came out of hiding and ran over to her mother, putting her arms around her mother's neck.

"Come over here with me, Destiny," Cameron said, taking her hand. He had a bad feeling and wanted to shield the kids from what he knew was going to be a dismal ending.

"Ma, I know you can hear me," Diamond

whispered, cradling her mother. But Mrs. O'Toole couldn't hear her daughter. A bullet entered her heart, killing her instantly. Diamond began rocking back and forth, not wanting to let go because she knew this would be the very last time she would ever hold her mother in her arms again.

Chapter Twenty-Seven

Forever In Our Hearts

"What happened to Brad?" Lyric questioned after they picked her up from her luxury apartment in Santa Monica.

"He really wanted to come, but at the last minute an emergency came up with another client," Kennedy explained.

"Oh." Lyric sounded unenthused, but Kennedy didn't mind. She knew how to win women like Lyric over. All she wanted was to be told how great she was.

"We've been getting tons of positive feedback about you. Brad has a ton of wonderful projects lined up for you."

"Really?! He didn't mention anything. I was thinking he wasn't pleased with my delivery on things... ya know," Lyric smacked. "I mean, he stay critiquing my clothes, my hair." Lyric rolled her eyes.

"Brad means no harm. He's over critical with everyone, including me."

"Fo'real?"

"Yes. I'm used to him now. But you're gorgeous and you look incredible in everything you wear so don't pay Brad any attention."

"Thank you, girl! It's hard being so beautiful and sexy. People constantly hate on you. I'm like don't be mad at me cause I'm a bad bitch," Lyric complained.

"One of the prices of fame, but you're doing an excellent job handling all the hate."

"You need to substitute for Brad more often. You understand me, unlike him."

"Thank you. I truly appreciate you saying that." Kennedy sounded extra humble and sincere.

"I can't put my finger on it, but you look so familiar to me."

"Both times we met at the office you said that," Kennedy said smiling. Kennedy had an idea why. When they initially met at her office a year ago she was in a baseball cap, no makeup, and sweats. Now she was polished and dressed professionally. But Kennedy was sure her voice and face did seem familiar to Lyric, but it was impossible for her to put those two different times together, which Kennedy preferred.

"I guess you just have one of those faces," Lyric said, brushing if off before taking a call. "Hello!"

"You know you a dead hoe." The male voice said then hung up.

"I'm sick of this motherfucker calling me!" Lyric tossed down her phone, pressing her lips together.

"Who is this motherfucker you speak of, if you don't mind me asking," Kennedy meddled.

"My ex-boyfriend, Packer. No matter how many times I change my phone number he keeps getting it."

"I'm sure he's still in love with you and wants you back."

A slight smile crept across Lyric's face. "I need to keep you around me all the time. You're great for my ego."

"I only speak the truth."

"You're probably right. Packer is in love with me, but he's served his purpose. If it wasn't for him, I wouldn't be where I am now."

"That's an odd statement to make especially since Brad told me you became an Internet sensation because of a sex video with an NBA superstar."

"Yeah, sexing fine ass Cameron Robinson did put me on the map, but if it wasn't for Packer that never would've happened. I guess I owe my initial success to him and Darcy."

Hmmm, I wonder how this Packer guy was the reason Lyric could hook up with Cameron? I want to delve deeper into that comment, but now that she's finally mentioned Darcy, I need to find out what I can, Kennedy thought to herself.

"Who is Darcy?" Kennedy felt it was best to pretend she was clueless as to who Darcy was.

"She was my first publicist. She brokered the release of the sex video. Darcy is quite crafty."

"You sound fond of her. Why did you stop working together?"

"No, I'm not. Darcy's uppity. She act like she better than me, but I was the one that kept her pockets full. I might've kept working with her, but her partner was a bigger asshole than her."

"So, you didn't like working with her partner?"

"I didn't exactly work with him. I guess he was more like a silent partner. They was also fuckin' too," Lyric added. "I only met him a few times because he lived in New York, but he would always make lil' rude comments to me. He acted like I was some two-dollar slut. I think the nigga just wanted to fuck me, what you think, Kennedy?"

"I think you're absolutely right. I'm sure this guy... what was his name again?"

"Michael something. I can't think of his last name."

"Yeah, that Michael guy definitely wanted to get with you. I'm sure Darcy is devastated she no longer has you as a client."

"For sure! She was pissed when I told her I was taking my business elsewhere. She even threatened to expose me... I mean." Lyric caught herself about to tell it and became silent.

"Lyric, you don't have to hold things back from me," Kennedy said giving Lyric a friendly pat on the arm. "We all have things we rather keep secret."

"Maybe we can talk about it later." Lyric nodded her head towards the driver. It was her way of letting Kennedy know she didn't trust spilling it all in front of him. "What I will say is yeah, Darcy has some dirt on me, but I have plenty on her too so we even. I went my way and she going hers. I'm sure she struggling though, cause she was always complaining I was the only client that paid like clockwork. That's because I'm about my business," Lyric boasted, snapping her fingers.

"Lucky for us, you're our client now."

"Yeah! I really like you, Kennedy. We should hang out sometime."

"I think that's a great idea. But first, let's go inside and get this interview and photo shoot done."

"I didn't even realize we were finally here. I'm ready though. Let's do this."

Kennedy was pleased with herself. She managed to befriend a woman that disgusted her and find out some interesting information about her nemesis, Darcy. Kennedy always suspected Darcy didn't have the money to pull off her heist and now she knew it was Blair's ex, Michael Frost, who had funded her scheme. Even with his financial help, Darcy was struggling and when the time was right, Kennedy would make her move to get back what was rightfully hers.

Only by the grace of God was Diamond able to function and make funeral arrangements for her mother. She wanted to crawl up in a ball and stay in bed all day, every day, so she could cry in peace. But not only did Diamond have to bury and mourn her mother, she had to be strong for Destiny and Elijah.

"I brought you some food from your favorite Dominican restaurant," Cameron said holding a white paper bag.

"I'm not hungry."

"Diamond, you've barely eaten these last few days. You need food to keep your strength up."

"I don't want to be strong. I just wanna sleep." Diamond pulled back the flat sheet and duvet cover on her bed. "All I need is a couple of hours to rest."

"Okay. I'll take the kids out for a while and you get some rest. If you want me to bring you anything back, give me a call." Cameron was about to walk out the door until he heard stifled weeping. When he turned back around, Diamond's face was buried in her hands. He rushed to her side and Diamond completely broke down.

"Why did they have to take my mother," Diamond bawled. "Not my mother," she continued to sob.

Cameron's muscular arms weren't even strong enough to hold up an emotionally shattered Diamond. He felt helpless when her limp body collapsed to the floor. "Baby, I know you're hurting, but we'll get through this together... I promise," Cameron said, speaking lovingly in Diamond's ear while gently stroking her hair.

Blair had gotten out the shower and was moisturizing her still damp skin when she heard a knock at the door. Thinking it was maid service coming to clean her hotel room, she ignored it, but the knocking persisted.

"Coming!" she called out before opening the door. "Kirk, what are you doing here?"

"I wanted to bring you this." Kirk handed her an envelope.

"You could've given this to Jillian," Blair said, taking it from his hand.

"I know, but I wanted to speak to you myself. I

told Jillian you wouldn't mind if she let me know the hotel you were staying at and the room number."

"You lied. I do mind."

"Blair, I know we're going through a rough time."

"You're suing me for custody of our son, that's more than a rough patch."

"You're trying to take my son to LA. I want him to stay in New York. He needs to be close to his father, not caught up in your Hollywood world."

"Kirk, if you came here to plead your case, I'm not interested. You should've done that before you unleashed your lawyer on me. Now, we'll leave it to the courts to decide." Blair started to shut the door in Kirk's face.

"Wait!" he shouted, putting his arm up to stop the door from closing. "I didn't come over here to discuss our custody case. It's about Diamond."

"What about her?"

"She really needs you right now, Blair. Cameron asked me to speak to you."

"When Diamond had you ask me to call her, I didn't then, and nothing has changed now."

"Something has changed. Diamond's mother got shot and killed recently," Kirk revealed.

"Mrs. O'Toole is dead?!" Blair became breathless. She let go of the door because she needed to sit down.

"Blair..." Kirk pushed the door open and came

into the hotel room. "Now you understand why you need to call Diamond. She's in a lot of pain."

"I can only imagine. They were so close." Blair then opened the envelope Kirk had given her and saw the invite to the funeral and memorial service. There was a beautiful picture of Mrs. O'Toole on one side and on the other, it said, "Forever in our Hearts", surrounded by rose petals. As Blair read over the details for the upcoming funeral she became flooded with grief.

"Can I tell Cameron that you'll be at the funeral?" Kirk questioned.

"I don't know," Blair said softly.

"What do you mean, you don't know! Diamond needs you. I guess this Hollywood fame has gone to your head and you no longer care about your real friends just your industry associates. You and Skee really do make the perfect couple after all."

"Like you really give a damn about what Diamond needs. You're only concerned about Cameron and what he wants. So, save your hypocritical judgment. We both know your moral compass is less than zero. You've delivered the message, now you can go." Blair stood up, walked over to the door and opened it.

"Fine, I'll leave. But I remember how much love you had for Diamond and if you put aside whatever went down between the two of you, I guarantee the love ain't gone nowhere. Think about it."

After Kirk left, Blair picked up her cell phone and her initial reaction was to call Diamond. She thought about it further and placed her iPhone back down. Blair loved Diamond, but a day didn't go by that she didn't replay the last argument between them. The words her best friend said cut deep and Blair wasn't sure she could ever get over it.

Packer was downstairs in the den, doing what he loved most... counting money. He normally preferred to do this alone or in the company of a woman because seeing money add up was a form of foreplay for him. It was a gateway to great sex or masturbation. Unfortunately for Packer, neither would be happening for him today. He did have company, but it was strictly business.

"You really fucked up." Packer shook his head with discontent.

"Man, I know, but I'ma make it right. We have everything covered and this time we won't miss."

"You bet not. A woman died and some kid got hurt because of ya's fuck up. And you still didn't hit yo' target."

"One of them niggas was excited to bust off and got trigger happy. We don't have to worry about him no more. He's been dealt wit'. I made sure he was put out of commission permanently."

"I would hate for the same thing to happen to you," Packer remarked, rubbing his fingers over a stack of bills.

"That ain't necessary. I told you, Cameron Robinson will be dealt with. We have everything planned out."

"Good. After he's out the way, Lyric is next."

"I'm on it. I won't let you down," the low-level henchman guaranteed.

"That's all I needed to know. I don't wanna hear nothing from you until it's done. Now get out." Packer dismissed his hired help and put his focus back on his first love… money.

Chapter Twenty-Eight

Déjà vu

"Thank you for coming with me. I couldn't have done this without you," Blair said, squeezing Skee's hand as they took a seat right when the service was about to begin. She briefly made eye contact with both Diamond and Kennedy before quickly looking away.

"Babe, don't be nervous. I know it was hard, but you did the right thing coming here to pay respect to Diamond's mother," Skee reassured her.

"Thank you." Blair didn't attend the church service, but she wanted to be at the cemetery before they lowered Mrs. O'Toole's casket in the ground. It would be her opportunity to say goodbye.

"I can't believe Blair and Kennedy both showed up," Diamond commented to Cameron.

"I told you they would." Cameron made sure of that because after he had Kirk speak to Blair he also spoke to her and Kennedy personally. Cameron didn't hold back. He explained it was imperative they show up and he meant it. He tried his best to be there for Diamond, but he knew she needed her best friends, both of them.

When the service was finally over, Kennedy was the first to get up and give her condolences to Diamond. "My heart breaks for you, Diamond. Your mother was an amazing woman and I know how much you loved her and she loved you. I'm so sorry." Kennedy reached out and gave Diamond a warm embrace.

"Do you mind if we turn this into a group hug?" Kennedy and Diamond turned around simultaneously and saw Blair standing in front of them.

"I think Kennedy would agree with me when I say this hug wouldn't be complete without you," Diamond said, smiling as the three women held on to each other tightly.

"I ain't gonna lie. I didn't think Blair was gonna show up," Kirk admitted. "Whatever you said to her, must've resonated.

"I had to make it happen. I couldn't watch my wife shut herself off from the rest of the world. I love her too much," Cameron stated.

"Sounds like you haven't given up on your marriage. Does that mean the divorce is off?" Kirk asked.

"It's for sure on hold for the time being. We'll see what happens. I'm taking things one day at a time."

"I hear you, man. I hope things work out for you. I couldn't save my relationship with Blair," Kirk said eyeing Skee. "But I think you and Diamond have a fighting chance."

"I know it must be hard seeing Blair with him." Cameron couldn't help but notice the look of death Kirk was giving Skee. "He ain't one of my favorite people either," he added.

"I don't understand what Blair sees in that asshole," Kirk scoffed. "I can't do anything about her moving to LA and being wit' him, but he won't be playing daddy to my son. I won't let that happen."

"I don't blame you. Donovan is your son. If Diamond and I do end up getting a divorce, she ain't gonna have no other man playing daddy to my kids. I'm the only father they know and it's gonna stay like that."

"I feel you. That's why I've prepared myself for a lengthy court battle to keep my son right here in New York, if that's what it takes," Kirk said, nodding.

"It'll work out. You ready to walk back over there with everybody else so we can head out,"

Cameron said looking at his watch, realizing it was time to go.

"Yep. Being around all this sadness and seeing nothing but the color black is wearing on my soul. Let's get outta here," Kirk agreed.

While the two men commenced to some small talk, they were oblivious to what was going on around them. Packer's hired goons had been lying in wait for the ideal time to make their move. This was it. Cameron had separated himself from the crowd and it was a clear shot to take him down.

The men seemed to blend in with the crowd since they were wearing all black too, but they weren't guests, they were killers. Diamond was the first to spot something was slightly off when she started looking around to find Cameron. There were three men who were all wearing black baseball caps pulled low over their eyes. She observed one of the men reaching into the back of his pants and pulling out what looked to be a gun.

Diamond sprinted off. Her kids were sitting down on the chairs with some family members. Kennedy and Blair were in deep conversation so at first, no one noticed what was going on until they were all startled by the deafening screams.

"Cameroooon!" Diamond howled as loud as she could, running towards him pointing her finger. "He has a gun!"

Cameron and Kirk both spun in the direction

Diamond was pointing. By the time they made eye contact with the shooters, guns were already raised. Both men dived to the ground, hearing the bullets ring in the air.

Dear God no! Not this again. Please... Please... Please don't do this to me. First, my mother, now Cameron. I'm begging you please, don't take my husband away from me too, Diamond pleaded, looking towards the sky for a sign that Cameron would survive.